AS TIM APPROACHES

(From Era to Era 1)

by

ANDREW HARRISON

Preface

Chris arrives in Xi'an, China. He needs time away from his home in England while he thinks through his relationship with Michelle. Now they have graduated from Chester University, should they get married? What will the future hold for them? Can they really settle down and live a normal life in a World plagued by earthquakes, disease and disaster?

The Watchers covertly observe the events worldwide; they are angels responsible for the welfare of the Chosen Ones, Chris being one of them. But will Michelle respond before it is too late?

This novel covers a period of fifteen years, from now until the end of the World as we know it, the end of our present era. The story follows the lives of Chris, Michelle and their families until the Great Removal of the Chosen Ones from the Earth. But will this event be a time of brilliant light, or a time of deep darkness?

I offer this novel to you with the hope that you will begin a voyage of discovery and engage with the many mysteries of life.

Andrew Harrison, 2018

Contents

Part 1

A LONG WAY FROM HOME

WATCHERS

Little do they know what's in store for them over the next few years. The world has experienced many things over the millennia, but here comes something new. Events will unfold that will pierce the soul of all creatures. Long has Creation endured the conflicts, greed and strife! Still, life continues to smooch into oblivion.

The heat will gradually increase until we see who comes out glowing from the refining fire.

CHAPTER 1

A Friendly Face

A young man stepped out of the airport terminal at Xi'an airport, wondering how on earth he was going to get to his hotel in the city centre. He was average height for an Englishman, but he still stood with a slouch. His hair swung over his left eye like a sort of cool pirate. This was his first visit to a hot country, and he was both apprehensive and excited at the same time. He felt a sudden blast of heat against his body.

"Can I help you?" The voice came from a young Chinese man who had seen the white foreigner looking confused.

"Err...thank you, who are you?"

"I'm a volunteer, a university student."

"Oh, I see," said the Englishman who was a few years older than the student. He had heard that Chinese people were friendly and helpful to visitors, so he decided to trust he was who he said he was.

"I was just wondering how to get to my hotel. It's at the Bell Tower. Do you know where that is?"

"Come this way please." The young Englishman felt like an honoured guest. "There's a bus take you straight to Zhong Lou."

"Sorry?" said the Englishman confused.

The university student also started to look confused, wondering why the foreigner said, 'sorry', but he had heard English people say 'thank you' a lot so thought the same must apply to 'sorry'.

The Englishman said, "Pardon, what did you say just then?"

"I'm sorry I don't understand, my English is not standard. You take the bus over here," said the university student with a slightly embarrassed smile.

"What do I say to the bus driver? Will he understand 'Bell Tower'?"

"Zhong Lou."

"Oh, that's what you said earlier. So, Zhong Lou is the Chinese for Bell Tower?"

"That's right. Wish you good time in China. Where you from?"

"England."

"Beautiful country."

"Oh! Have you been?" said the Englishman thinking he may have something in common with his Chinese companion after all. 'I wonder which part he's been to, perhaps the Lake District,' he thought.

"No...It's not easy for me."

"Oh! I'm sorry to hear that. Thank you for your help anyway, you've been very helpful."

"It's my pleasure."

That last phrase didn't seem quite right to the Englishman, although he understood it of course. 'I know,' he thought, 'We usually say 'My pleasure' without the 'it's', or 'It's a pleasure' without the 'my'; or do we?'

Anyway, he thought the student's English was quite good. He could certainly communicate well enough. He wondered if all Chinese university students could speak the same level of English. This interested him because he was considering teaching English in a Chinese university in the future.

The volunteer guided him to the Airport Bus ticket desk and did all the talking to the two shyly smiling attendants. The student got permission to sit with the young Englishman in the waiting lounge.

Just outside the waiting section, building work was underway behind partitions. Inside the waiting area, the seats were dotted with Chinese of all ages, but it wasn't too busy. There were two wide screen TVs. A Chinese family were watching a Chinese soap on one, while a group of young men were watching football on the other. Attractive dark blue glazed pots stood on the floor at strategic points containing what looked like palm branches reaching over six feet in the air. 'Not bad,' he thought.

They sat near Gate 46 for the bus to Zhong Lou. Eventually, the doors opened and the bus parked ready to receive passengers.

"If you have any problem in China you can call me."

"Okay, thank you". The Englishman was surprised at how friendly his companion was, but he also felt a bit uncomfortable and thought, 'Surely, he's not actually going to give me his phone number!' To his surprise, the student got out his phone and gave him his number. The Englishman was a bit anxious to get on his way in case the bus left, but the student was in no hurry. Out of politeness the Englishman didn't rush him and said, "My name's Chris by the way, nice to meet you."

"My name is Wang Bin, but you can call me Waiting."

"Waiting?"

"Yes."

"Okay, well I'll be on my way." He turned to leave.

"How to spell Chris?"

"How do you spell Chris? C.H.R.I.S," he answered, trying not to sound too brusque in his anxiety to get away.

"Have a good trip!"

'There he goes again', thought Chris. 'I'm at the destination of my trip. Shouldn't it be, 'Have a good time'? No, that's if you're going to a party. 'Have fun!' Maybe in a metaphorical sense, if we were close friends. 'All the best!' is a possibility, or just repeating, 'Nice meeting you!' Or, 'Hope it goes well!'" This English teaching idea wasn't going to be as straight forward as he thought, although Chris felt quite up for the challenge.

He boarded the bus easily and gave a quick wave back to Waiting. The cool air in the bus was wonderful. He wasn't used to air-conditioned coaches. He sat towards the back on one of the mid-blue coloured reclining seats. There was even a loo situated below a small TV screen. He wondered if anyone would actually dare to use it.

The bus filled to half its capacity before it set off. Chris wondered how he was going to work out where to get off, but then he remembered the Bell Tower was the last stop, so he didn't worry about it. He noticed the young lady sat in front of him release the back of her seat into the reclining position without checking behind her. Perhaps it was common for Chinese to do this, but he still gave a quick glance behind him before he followed suit.

Chris closed his eyes. He was very tired and the events of the last twenty four hours flicked through his brain. Ironically, this trip to China was his chance to clear his head for four weeks, not cloud it further. This break was to be a turning point in his life, or a decisive entry into adulthood. Even though he had four weeks to reflect, his brush with China and its different climate and culture had somehow awakened his senses in a way he couldn't explain. He had already heard that China was a place of contradictions. Things were moving rapidly yet at the same time everyone seemed as laid back as the lady sat in front of him. It was going to be a real culture shock. On the other hand, Chris was not used to such innocent friendliness in such a big city and found it refreshing. If the same friendliness were shown in London or another big city it would set off alarm bells. Are all Chinese like this? Or, are Chinese only friendly to foreigners?

Chris drowsed for about half an hour and woke up to the issues he had to think through on his holiday (or perhaps he should call it a retreat). He thought about Michelle his fiancee, whom he started going out with at university during his teacher training. On the surface, they seemed to be set for married life together. But he wanted to know for sure. They loved each other, without a doubt, and enjoyed being together. They even had plans for children in the future, in a secure home with Chris pursuing his teaching career. He already had a full-time teaching job lined up in Berkshire for September.

Chris remembered his holiday with Michelle in Keswick, climbing Cat Bells Fell together and looking down over Derwent Water through the mist. That moment had sealed their relationship. They both knew they wanted to spend the rest of their lives together.

Then he was reminded of something that at times felt like a brick wall between them, an insurmountable wall with no solution in sight.

*

Meanwhile, it was morning in Winchester, England, and Chris' fiancee Michelle tried to put on her make-up. Sat up in front of the mirror in her night clothes, she ran through every moment of her relationship with Chris again and again. Should she have been different? Is she not good enough for him? Could she have been a better companion, a better girlfriend? Was it just a university romance and now she had to face the real world? But she had no contingency plans, everything she had planned involved Chris. What if he decided to break off the relationship? She was not going to let that happen! But at the end of the day she was powerless to influence his decision. They had both agreed on this space to think things through.

'What's wrong with me, I can have anyone I want. I'm attractive, have loads of friends, I get on well with everyone.....but I don't

14

want just anyone, I want Chris! I feel so happy and secure with him. He is such a decent man but at the same time not stuffy or geeky. He's intelligent, he has strong beliefs – and arms – but he's not arrogant like other men...and I LOVE HIM!'

*

Chris sat on his hotel bed switching the seventy or so channels. He found some news being read in English on one of the CCTV channels. He was shocked to hear the 'breaking news' about a Russian earthquake. So far, the initial death toll figures were five hundred thousand. He wondered if it was a mistake in translation. In fact he was sure it must be. They didn't seem to have any pictures available yet so he turned it off and decided to check the news again the next day. Or, if he was miraculously over his jet lag before then he would check his computer and send Michelle an email at the same time. An agitated sleep overtook him again, but it was sleep nonetheless.

*

Michelle dried her eyes with a piece of tissue, unable to finish doing her make-up. In the bedroom mirror she could see the reflection of her whole childhood through to her tumultuous teens. She saw the cuddly toys, Winnie the Pooh, Eeyore and her favourite teddy, all with memories of their own. Her CD collection had been gathering dust while she had been at university. She was at the beginning of something new and in her heart she saw only two possibilities: a happy life with Chris or a miserable life without him. She couldn't bear to think about option two. If she believed in a god she would pray, but she didn't believe in anything like that. She just felt lost.

Mum knocked on the door to ask if she wanted to go to the shops after lunch. She thought that was a good idea, pulled herself together, dried her eyes and added a little more make-up.

That afternoon, in her English home town of Winchester, she fell back into her teenage shopping routine she had during her High School days. She became her Mum's teenage daughter all over again, but this time a bit more polite towards her parents, meaning very stroppy instead of a complete pain in the neck!

At about 3 o'clock they decided to have a coffee somewhere. They chose Dunelm. The ground floor was large and stuffed with household products. Michelle wanted to have a look round after coffee because it was her Mum's birthday in a week's time. They walked up the stairs to the second floor which was smaller and served as a balcony looking over the ground floor.

As they stood at the counter rail choosing a cake to go with their drink, Michelle began to feel dizzy and sickly. Everything appeared blurred, like a fuzzy tunnel. Her legs were turning to jelly. She saw her Dad at the counter ordering tea for two and a cappuccino, but he looked too distant to call out to. She felt her Mum's hand on her shoulder, "Are you alright?"

"No, I feel strange. I'm sorry I've got to sit down."

"I'll join you in a minute," Mum reassured her.

Dad carried the drinks and cakes on a tray over to their table. "I got you a scone, I don't know if that's what you wanted."

"That's fine Dad, thanks."

"How are you feeling now?" asked Mum.

"Not too bad, still a little bit shaky."

"Well, here's your cappuccino. Hope it doesn't make you feel worse."

"It won't."

"Maybe it's the time of the month," Mum suggested.

"Yeah, maybe," said Michelle knowing she was probably just stressed over Chris. 'What if he finds someone else in China?' she thought, but knowing he wasn't really like that.

"Did you read about the Winchester earthquake while you were at university?" Dad interjected.

"Pardon? Oh, a joke, well done Dad! I know you don't get earthquakes in England."

"That's a myth," said Dad, "We just don't usually feel them. You ought to know that, being a scientist!"

"I'm not a scientist," snapped Michelle feeling irritable. "Anyway, I studied Biology, not Earth Sciences!"

Dad got up and went to the counter to ask for some more milk for the tea.

"So how bad was the earthquake then?" asked Michelle.

"Oh not too bad, the funny thing was everyone in Winchester

16

actually felt it," said Mum.

Michelle started to worry about Chris again. 'What if there's a big earthquake like the one in Sichuan or the massive one a long time before that?' she thought anxiously. Mum realised it wasn't the best topic to talk about in the circumstances so she changed the subject. "Is Chris skyping you today?"

"I don't know. He doesn't know whether he'll be able to get onto the internet. He said he'll either send me an email or a text somehow to arrange something."

"It'll be a bit difficult won't it, with the time difference."

"Yes, it's seven hours in the Summer, so I'll probably speak to him one afternoon when it's night time for him."

Michelle thought to herself, 'Little does Mum know the torment I'm going through. I can't begin to explain it all to her, she probably wouldn't understand anyway.' Mum wondered if Michelle was ever going to open up, share her worries and actually admit she had feelings. She didn't want to push it in case Michelle thought she was interfering and she started ranting again.

Dad couldn't face the whole emotion of it, so he just went through the motions of being 'Dad', suppressing his anxiety for his daughter whom he loved deeply. He wouldn't trust any man who took an interest in her anyway. He imagined her university lover stood on a rocky mountain, an earthquake ripping it apart, huge rocks and boulders crumbling, the noise deafening, and her boyfriend screaming for dear life as he fell down into a bottomless cavern, his limbs being severed off one by one against jagged edges on descent. All that remained was a head with mouth open wide and horrified eyes staring up at him through the darkness, getting smaller and smaller until it had completely disappeared ... And he hadn't even met him yet!

WATCHERS

So much darkness is emerging. Things are ripe for fulfilment. Relationships will start to become more and more brittle and fall apart.

Let's keep a close watch on them; we have a responsibility to protect the chosen ones until their deliverance. They will need patience and endurance. They will feel abandoned. Peace of mind and heart will be available for only a few.

CHAPTER 2

A Spectacular Performance

They were an 'average' family living in Albert Town, Jamaica. Joe was in the town centre unable to get out of a business meeting. His boss had insisted he stay behind, but all he could think of was being with his wife at the hospital. His two daughters from his previous marriage were at their friends' house for the night, having been relieved of their chores while Edwina was in hospital.

Edwina had been taken into hospital with contractions just in case it wasn't a false alarm again. Joe, her husband, had been phoning every hour or so, but he was misinformed about his wife. He was given the impression that Edwina was comfortable and contraction free, sitting up in bed and sipping cool lemonade. He was waiting for another opportunity to phone, but unbeknown to him, his wife was in labour already.

Sister Lucy suddenly panicked when she realised Edwina had been in labour for twenty minutes. "Quick! What's Mr. Oliver's telephone number?"

"I don't know!" replied her colleague in the middle of the proceedings, "Push now, push!"

*

Joe Oliver sat at the board meeting table with a false smile, pretending to listen attentively to every word about the business development plans. He nodded his head with a knowing smile every time he thought it was appropriate, but unfortunately he eventually got it wrong as he caught himself nodding and smiling while everyone was looking directly at him with a confused face. He was saved by the tea boy who coyly entered the room in a state of quiet panic. "Errr, Mr. Oliver has a phone call."
Joe jerked up too quickly and knocked his papers on the floor to his embarrassment. He fumbled to pick them up under the silent staring eyes. Sweat poured from his face as he unceremoniously dumped the pile on the table mumbling 'sorry' as he left the room. His boss simply sat there with a pathetic grin on his face, his eyes following his employee as he stumbled out of the room.

The new creation exercised its healthy pair of lungs, inhaling the delivery room air for the first time, clenching his unusually large fists. The baby's exhausted mother lay almost lifeless on the blood stained bed. Her ordeal was over and began to fade as she looked upon this miracle of life.

*

Meanwhile, Joe was stuck in traffic in his bashed in old Aston, delayed by a ramshackled truck in the middle of the road with four men struggling to replace a wheel. The only thing blowing his horn seemed to achieve was to make the men even more annoyed and confused.

*

"What a good pair of lungs he's got!" It was Nurse Mamosa barging into the room. She was actually a neighbour of Edwina's and lived on the same street. She had popped round to her home from time to time to check on her during her pregnancy.

Mamosa had jet black skin and chubby features. Her body was fat and sweaty, with bracelets eating into her flesh. Her magnetic necklace was so desperate to let go it squeaked every time she spoke. Her accent was broad Jamaican, unlike Joe and Edwina, who were both from Jewish descent, having emigrated to Jamaica as teenagers with their parents. Both their fathers had been promoted in the same clothes manufacturing company at the same time, so with a sense of adventure, and because they were already good friends, they decided to move their entire families to the Caribbean together.

After Joe's first wife and mother of his two daughters died in the crossfire of a Yardie Gang shoot out on Kingston Harbour, Edwina helped him to bring up his daughters. She had been Joe's childhood sweetheart and she became like a second mother to the girls. Now, they had their own baby son.

"What you callin'im den?" asked Mamosa.

"Oh, Christaff...Christaff Young."

"Christaff Young Oliver?"

"Yes."

"You givin'im a proper namin' dough!"

"What do you mean?" Edwina was curious to know what she meant although she could have done without having a full-scale conversation after having just given her whole energy to bringing forth a new life.

"You know, a ceremony an'all!"

"We haven't decided yet. We were going to have a party after it was born, but..."

"Don't you worry, I'll arrange everythin'. I know a really good spirit doctor can put a blessin'on'im. He needs a good start in life."

Edwina was too exhausted to have a debate and it was the last thing on her mind when she saw Joe coming through the doorway out of breath.

"You're a bit late, but don't panic, we got everythin' under control. I'll leave you and Edwina to look at Christaff together," Mamosa said as she walked out of the room.

Edwina looked up at her husband and spoke with a quiet hoarse voice: "Say hello to your son."

"Hi there, you're a whopper!"

"He's got giant hands like you."

"He's got your beautiful round eyes," said Joe kissing Edwina on the forehead.

*

Eventually, it was time to head home.

Joe drove his wife and their new arrival home. "How about a bit of Bob Marley from my playlist," he said.

"Okay, I suppose he's going to have to get used to your obsession with Reggae eventually."

As Edwina listened to the music, she recalled the words of Nurse Mamosa. What did she mean by spirit doctor? What type of doctor is that? Joe and Edwina had talked about a religious ceremony for baby Christaff before he was born, but hadn't seen it as much of a priority, even though they were both Jewish and they started life in Israel. But they concluded they would probably talk it through with a local Rabbi when the child was born, if they felt the inclination to. After all, they had not stepped into a synagogue since they stepped into Jamaica.

The Ceremony

They decided to go with Mamosa's suggestion. They had talked it through the night before, and because they were novices in the area of spiritual things they thought they would go for the easy option. They had enough to do getting used to having a new little fellow around, and Nurse Mamosa did tell them she would organise everything.

Mamosa brought round her spirit doctor friend that morning. He had two fairly large bags with him containing the regalia he needed for the ceremony. Joe and Edwina acted politely even though they were a little bit apprehensive. Their two daughters were even more apprehensive, but they quietly watched the performance take its course. And what a performance! The spirit doctor was dressed in feathers and snakes all over his dark skin. He picked up Christaff in both hands while his own body shook and vibrated in time with his barely musical mumbled incantations which were unintelligible to the Olivers. This continued for fifteen minutes.

Christaff's Papa and Mama's hearts sank as they saw this rank spectacle. That was their child he was holding! Edwina glanced over to Mamosa to read her expression. She didn't look concerned, but instead gleeful.

The grotesque visitor eventually laid Christaff on a rug he had previously placed on the sitting room floor. The baby was placed in the middle of a five pointed star which had a lit candle at each point. The spirit doctor finally pulled a large necklace from his neck. It had a furry container like a horn. He opened it, knelt down and began to pour out red liquid over baby Christaff's face. Edwina thought it was going into Christaff's mouth so she yelped, "No...stop it!"

Drops of blood fell upon the baby's forehead and chin as the spirit doctor and Mamosa laughed in unison. Chuckling, the spirit doctor said, "Don't worry, all finished. He's a fine child."

Edwina and Joe found themselves rushing their guests out of their home.

"Why did we ever allow that freak in here! We should have gone to the Rabbi," sobbed Edwina.

"I'm sorry, I should have listened to my doubts."

"You know I'm fragile … I have just had a baby you know!"

"I know you've had a baby … OUR baby!"

"You're supposed to take the lead! How can I trust you?"

"Look, I know you are fragile and neurotic, but it was your idea …."

Edwina ran into the bedroom and slammed the door while the girls sat together crying.

The baby had remained in a deep sleep during the ceremony and the argument. The Oliver family didn't know whether that was a good thing or a bad thing, but assumed it was the safest.

By the time evening came, they had made up and the girls were out with friends. But there was a tangible atmosphere in the house. They didn't think much of it and although it was a struggle to concentrate on things, at the back of their minds they thought it was simply their distress over the mistake they had made, and the aftermath of their argument. Somehow they managed to make plans for inviting their friends round for a party to celebrate Christaff's arrival. Neither of them had any idea what effect the ceremony had had on their baby boy. After all, he had been asleep all the way through the ceremony!

*

Christaff's baby mind replayed that ceremony again and again as he slept in his cot in the nursery. His sleep was deep and trancelike, but his eyelids quivered as his eyeballs twitched irritably under the skin. Christaff's thoughts were analytical and developing. He could visualise the shaman-like character shaking rattles and wearing a costume depicting snakes of various colours and sizes. The spirit doctor had cows' horns protruding from his temples. The dark face with eyes wide open stared into Christaff's soul, a meeting of spirits that would define the baby's whole life.

In the morning, the baby awoke to the sound of a deafening, African-style drum beat in his fragile skull, ever growing in speed and intensity. Christaff's eyes shot open and his mouth gave out a piercing scream that reverberated round every room in the house.

"What's that?" said Edwina with panic in her voice.

"I don't know. It can't be Christaff, it didn't sound like a baby...I'll go and check."

Joe tiptoed into the nursery. Christaff was lying on his back, with wide eyes planted into his tiny red sweaty face. The baby's Papa placed his hand onto Christaff's chest and gently shook him. No response, but he could feel his son's little heart pounding and racing faster than he thought was possible. "Edwina!" he shouted. She rushed to the nursery, "What! Christaff, what's wrong?"

Together, they took him to their bed and nursed him until he fell asleep and his heart stopped pounding. But from that time on they deeply regretted having Mamosa's friend at their house.

That afternoon, Edwina saw Mamosa while she was out shopping. They glanced at each other briefly, but Edwina avoided her. Mamosa didn't appear bothered by that, and in fact when Edwina gave another quick glance in Mamosa's direction, she noticed the nurse chuckling to herself as though she had expected there to be a rift between them and was actually pleased about it.

WATCHERS

It's begun. The Beast is taking root. Things are set in motion for the Battle of battles, but there is much to be fulfilled before that.

Sooner or later the Beast will take an interest in Israel. We must stay aware of the Olivers' plans and how much the child influences their decisions.

CHAPTER 3

News From Afar

"Hi darling, how's it going? Are you missing me?" said a smiling Michelle, so happy to see her boyfriend's face again in spite of being thousands of miles apart.

"Of course not … only kidding!"

"That's not funny!"

"I'm sorry, you know I'm missing you. What've you been up to?"

"Oh partying with my friends every night, buying expensive clothes and stuffing my face with chocolate," joked Michelle.

"Alright, alright, I said I was sorry!"

"But it's true … well all except for the 'partying and buying expensive clothes' bit."

"Well save some chocolate for me, you can't get chocolate I like here. They do have it, but it's...different."

"Chocolate will melt in the sun anyway, so it's probably best."

"I arranged to see a Chinese student called 'Waiting' the other day. We went for a walk in Qujiang park."

"I know," said Michelle. "I watched you."

"Oh of course, I thought I saw you hiding behind a tree," said Chris.

"No, I was watching you on my iPad, I carry it round with me. I can see all over China with it."

"I see … new brand is it? What's it called...'PINEapple'?"

"Oh you are soooooo funny! Who is this 'Waiting' then?"

"I met him at the airport. He's a student volunteer during the holidays."

"Waiting for you was he?"

"Ha ha. No, but he waited with me in the waiting lounge while I waited for the bus. Not much of a wait though."

"Don't get me stressed or I'll start losing 'weight'."

"Better stuff your face with chocolate then!"

They eventually stopped the ridiculously thin sarcasm, and instead shared how much they were missing each other. Michelle didn't have much to report. What she wanted to say was, 'WELL, DO YOU WANT ME OR NOT?' But she had to trust him to make up his own mind and tell her after the four weeks were over.

At the end of their conversation she declared, "I love you so much!"

Chris replied, "I love you so much too. I always will."

Michelle had to remind herself this was not his decision, it was just his feelings. "Shall we speak again in four days like we decided?"

Chris said, "Yes," but added, "If you need to speak earlier for any reason it's okay," half hoping she would break the rule they had made, rather than him.

"No, don't worry, let's stick to our plan. Well, let's try to anyway."

"At least we can text now! I've bought a Chinese phone and SIM card, and have just about worked out how to use it."

"That's great, I love you."

"Love you too. Say hi to your Mum and Dad."

"Will do."

They eventually switched off their computers. They both felt tearful as they got up from their seats thousands of miles apart, but in their hearts they were in the same room.

*

"Computers are an amazing thing. You can be at completely opposite ends of the earth and still talk to each other and see each other." Michelle's Mum's words were halted by a shaking. Everything in the living room became animated. Michelle and her Mum held onto their seats in shock. The rumbling and jingling sounds increased and the clock fell off the wall crashing to the floor. Both of them tensed their whole bodies as they gripped tightly to their chairs worried somehow that they may go shooting into the air or crashing to the floor like the clock.

The rumbling and shaking subsided, but countless car alarms created a din. As some of the alarms stopped they could hear distant sirens from emergency vehicles emerging from the noise.

When Michelle and her Mum eventually composed themselves, they looked at each other, confused. "This is England! What's going on?" muttered Michelle.

"This one was a bit worse than the other one I told you about."

"That's not very reassuring! I need a coffee, shall I make us one?" offered Michelle.

"Yes okay."

"That's if the kitchen's still there."

"Don't give me any sugar though, I'm on a diet. Second thoughts, double the sugar content for the shock."

"Any excuse! Double sugar coming up," said Michelle as she tentatively left the room for the kitchen.

*

It wasn't that simple for Jinny and Frank McCleod who were about to get onto their train at Glasgow Central Station. Their train had been right in front of them, but it derailed before their eyes in the hugest earthquake in Britain's known history. Girders had fallen round them and blood could be seen in every direction mixed in with the dust and debris. Ambulances could be heard in the distance but they were presumably not heading for them as their phones couldn't get a signal.

Survivors tried to comfort the wounded in whatever way they could think of. Some people were screaming out prayers and curses beside the dead and the dying. The devastation was interspersed with occasional hysterical people of various ages running through the rubble stained with blood.

The whole of the city of Glasgow was like a war zone with black smoke rising and filling the air. The Renfrewshire village of Houston near Glasgow airport was no exception. Survivors made their way to the village kirk where worshippers had been gathered just hours before. The Minister decided to turn them away as the internal walls were severely cracked. He feared an aftershock would trigger the church's collapse. So, those with cars decided to see if the roads were clear enough to take the wounded to hospital.

*

Unaware of the severity of the earthquake, Michelle and her Mum decided to get some 'retail therapy' in Salisbury and then make their way to Stonehenge which Michelle had only visited once when she was seven years old.

"Hey, I wonder if the stones have fallen over!" joked Michelle as they drove into the car park.

*

As they stood near the ancient structure they talked about the progress of humankind. "How did they get those stones on top of each other?" mused Mum.

"With great difficulty."

"How is it that something like this stands for thousands of years and yet our house is falling apart?"

"Why? What's wrong with it?"

"Didn't Dad tell you? The foundations need strengthening again."

"Well we'll just have to move house then won't we?" suggested Michelle.

"Where to?" Mum looked bemused.

"Stonehenge of course."

"Oh I see … yes, good idea," responded Mum sarcastically, adding, "We might get a bit wet though."

A sudden burst of 'Michelle, Ma Belle' by the Beatles attracted their attention.

"Oh I just got a text."

"Who from?"

"Chris."

"What does he say?"

"'Heard about earthquake. U alright?' How did he hear about that? It wasn't bad enough to be on Chinese telly was it?" Michelle texted him a reply to say it was nothing to worry about but they were moving house to Stonehenge. Chris ignored the joke and sent her a message saying, 'Glasgow destroyed. Was worried. Ur Auntie and Uncle OK?'.

"What does he say?" asked Mum. Michelle started to read the text to her Mum, but before she could finish it everything around her seemed to spin. When she came round she was on a stretcher being lifted into the back of an ambulance.

*

Meanwhile, Jinny and Frank McCleod stumbled across the platform which now bore no resemblance to what it was a few hours ago. A few hours before, it was a different world, one that was full of joy, sadness, breaking and forming of relationships, making business deals, casual chatter, families, singles, lonely people, the elderly, the disabled, the successful, all with their routines, their homes, their gardens. All this was now obliterated into a grey dusty mess spanning right across the largest city in Scotland. To the Glaswegians this was now a new world, one they hadn't anticipated when they ate their breakfast or dashed out of their houses first thing that morning. They now had to immediately develop a new state of mind with a whole new set of values.

Some survivors scurried around caring for themselves, trying to find help and a way out of the nightmare. Others selflessly attended to the wounded. Some just held the hands of the dying, not knowing what else they could do. Others tried to recall their First Aid training from yesteryears and offered the best help they could.

The McCleods fell into the first category, until they saw a boy of about seven years old walking gradually closer to them. His screams were intermittent as he came nearer. The closer he got the louder and more disturbing it became. The McCleods were moved with compassion for the little traumatised boy. They called over to him to ask his name but he continued making the same sound, as though he was trying to shout 'Mum' but only managing the first letter. Jinny crouched down and put her arm round the extremely pale child who ceased walking although he continued to stare ahead screaming into nothingness.

*

Michelle's Mum couldn't get through to Jinny and Frank on the phone so feared the worst. She didn't call Chris as she had enough to worry about caring for Michelle who was still very pale.

When she came round Michelle was feeling shaken and confused. Her life was in turmoil: earthquakes, missing relatives, being thousands of miles away from her fiance, on whom she had based her whole future, and who might ditch her! Everything seemed to be happening at once. When was this nightmare ever going to end?

*

31

Back in China, Chris however, slept twelve hours straight. He didn't even hear the text message he received from Waiting inviting him to meet him at Qujiang Park again.

*

In the nursery in Jamaica, the atmosphere felt oppressive and heavy, like the feeling you get when a thunderstorm is due, but this was worse as it permeated the Olivers' heart and soul. The couple looked down at their baby boy in his cot. His eyes stared up at them as though he knew everything they were thinking.

"Do you think he's alright … normal?" asked Edwina.

Joe looked down at his son, "I've got no idea."

WATCHERS

Earthquakes will continue to increase, so will disease, famine, desolation, and death by wild beasts. Livestock will diminish and many lives will be lost. Peace will leave the world and it won't only be wars they need to worry about, it will be the members of their own household who will betray them. Many of them will fall away from their Creator and turn to false prophets and gods.

The nations secretly despise those of The Way because they dare to proclaim a message warning them of Judgement. Soon the nations will react.

Part 2

A STRANGE CONNECTION

CHAPTER 4

Waiting's Cousin

Qujiang Park, located in the south of the city, was a popular destination for the people of Xi'an. They came from outlying areas to walk round the peaceful lake, see the grass, trees, and the sculptures representing the Tang Dynasty. It had been Chris' favourite destination over the last couple of weeks. It wasn't far from the Big Wild Goose Pagoda, a Buddhist tower in Da Ci'en Temple. The pagoda was over sixty metres high. It had even survived a massive earthquake in the Ming Dynasty which killed over 830 000 people. When Waiting told him this the other day, Chris began to consider the possibility that the Russian earthquake had been as bad as the news report conveyed after all.

Chris would often go for a walk alongside the lake and sometimes sit on a rock beside the long grasses to think about the future.

His first visit to the park had been a couple of days after arriving in Xi'an. His companion had been the student volunteer who met him at the airport. This time however he was walking with Waiting's sister whom he expected was actually his cousin. Chris had arranged to meet his friend at the park again by the giant balloon, but that same day Waiting had phoned to say he had something to do and could his sister meet him instead to practise her English. Chris reasoned he owed Waiting a favour for the help he gave at the airport, so he felt too guilty to say no.

Zhang Lili, whose English name was Lily, wanted to know about the culture in the UK, but Chris, overwhelmed by the recent global events as well as his own problems, spoke of the many tragedies that had been happening throughout the world, especially the Glasgow earthquake and how his fiancee's auntie and uncle had been caught up in it.

"Why you choose China for travelling?" said Lily wanting to get to know the young Englishman.

"I want to teach here in the future."

"You are teacher in China now?"

"No, in a few years."

"How long you teach in China?"

Chris wasn't quite sure if she understood what he was saying. He added, "I've got a job in England."

"Why you don't teach in China now?" Waiting's cousin asked. Feeling a bit awkward Chris repeated, "Because I have a job in China.....I mean England."

Waiting's cousin was likewise confused so she changed the subject quickly because she didn't want him to disappear. "Where are your English friends?" she asked.

"I came to China on my own. My girlfriend is back in England."

"Your girlfriend is gone back to England? Why?"

"No, she's not GONE back, she IS back in England."

"When will she arrive China?"

Chris was wondering whether this was helping either of them but he didn't want to disappoint, so he persisted. Waiting's cousin wanted to know more about Chris and wished he spoke some Chinese. Surely he had practised some Chinese before he travelled thousands of miles to another country!

Chris didn't really want to dwell on this topic with a stranger but thought he would outline it all for her. He took a deep breath, "My girlfriend is my fiancee, we're going to get married, but we've decided to have four weeks apart to think about things."

"Oh, you need a rest while your girlfriend prepares for the wedding, I know."

"There is something we have to think through."

"Think...through," she repeated.

"There's a problem. I believe in God but she doesn't."

"Oh, I hear all foreigner believe God. My grandparents believe Buddhinism."

"You mean Buddhism. I'm a Christian so I need to marry a Christian."

Waiting's cousin didn't know much about the topic, but asked him, "Do you been to church in Xi'an?"

"Have I been to church here? No, not yet."

They continued to attempt discussions on various topics such as belief, food and fashion. The language barrier made things difficult, but if Waiting's cousin hadn't known any English, then it would have been completely impossible, as Chris knew nothing of the Chinese language.

Michelle's Recovery

While in hospital, Michelle had had a series of tests after her collapse, but nothing untoward was found. Everyone put it down to her being anxious about an uncertain future after having completed her Degree. But the qualification meant nothing to her at the moment and she even considered not attending the awards ceremony at Chester Cathedral. In a way, she wished she had some sort of temporary illness so she could get a little bit of 'TLC' and get her mind off Chris. These four weeks were agony for her.

Jinny and Frank

The survivors of the Glasgow earthquake were evacuated to various places, including the poor orphaned child Jinny and Frank had rescued. Jinny and her husband made plans to stay indefinitely in their second home, a villa in France. In the meantime, they were invited to live with Michelle and her parents in Winchester.

Frank was unable to come to terms with recent events, not only the earthquake, but the child they came across and looked after amongst other things. Frank had always thought of himself as a good person, a good citizen with principles, but he had been shaken into seeing himself in a true light. Perhaps on balance he was a good citizen and a good person, but he had hidden behind his comforts. Subconsciously, he had considered that when other people had serious problems in life, for example a serious illness without adequate insurance or existing in war zones and political turmoil, it was somehow their own fault. This theory didn't work anymore. He had to face reality; the rain falls on the good and bad alike. His normal, stable, decent lifestyle had actually been a selfish smokescreen for his arrogance. At the moment, it looked like Jinny was going to have to aid his recovery. She was also aware of their past failings, but couldn't allow it to affect her as much. She was very pragmatic and was needed by her husband at this time.

WATCHERS

So far, England is holding on. They are feeling the pinch of the escalating tribulations. Most of the human race are oblivious to the issues surrounding the increasing pressures. Some will see the light as a consequence, but others will become bitter and fall away.

CHAPTER 5

Cheshire Cat

Before her auntie and uncle arrived in Winchester, Michelle took the opportunity to show her parents round Chester, her university town. As her parents always seemed to be busy, they had never stayed the night in Chester on their rare visits during her studies. Instead, Michelle either visited home or went with Chris to stay with his family during university holidays. Mum and Dad had promised to spend a few nights there sometime, but as usual they broke their promise. This was the only chance Michelle would get. Chester had become a haven of wonderful memories and she was sad to leave when her studies came to an end. Anyway, she wanted to show her Mum and Dad the city walls. Chester city walls had been a defensive structure built to protect the city in the past. Construction had been started by the Romans between 70 and 80 AD. After the Norman Conquest, their structure surrounded the whole of the medieval city. It was now a major tourist attraction with a two mile walkway.

As Michelle and her parents walked along a section of the wall, they could see it was blocked off ahead where the wall was being repaired. A tree branch leant over close to where they were walking. They heard a strange sound, a cross between a cat's meow and a growl. Looking to their right they saw a dishevelled grey cat looking ready to pounce. They moved slightly to the left and didn't think much of it. "Poor thing!" said Michelle walking on.

A couple of moments later they heard a growling screech. On turning round they saw Dad, his face twisted in agony. "Arghhh! Get it off me!" screamed Dad. The cat had jumped onto his back. Dad writhed around trying to shake the cat off his back, but it clung into his flesh with its claws piercing his shirt. Its teeth were also firmly gripped into the muscle in his shoulder and it became like an extension of his body.

"Get it off! Get it off! Arghh!" Mum tried to hit it off with her handbag, but knew that was useless. Michelle got out a nail file and repeatedly stabbed the cat. It still remained firm.

Eventually, passers-by ran to the rescue, and a stocky tanned and tattooed local grabbed the cat from under its belly and pulled as hard as he could, something the others had avoided doing in case it ripped Dad's flesh to shreds. What remained of the cat in his hands he immediately threw over the wall before it could do the same again. The remaining mass of fur and flesh wriggled in the grass and was immediately attacked by an army of black beetles.

Dad lay exhausted on his stomach, sobbing in great pain. Michelle got tissues out and started to use them to remove the fur and teeth from her Dad's back.

The tattooed man quickly wiped the blood off his hands and called the ambulance. "We'd better all go to hospital in case we've caught rabies or something!" said Bill.

*

In Xi'an, Mr. Harrison had heard his daughter's friend Chris was coming to China, so he arranged for him to have a go at teaching his Chinese English Major students and afterward join in with a game of English-style Rounders that he had introduced to his students several years before. They had even established their own rules, a version of the game that they found to be workable and appropriate for Chinese university students. They named the game 'Chang'an Rounders'. This was found to be an apt title as Xi'an used to be called Chang'an in the past, when it was the capital of China. 'Chang'an' means 'eternal peace'. However, the game was all but peaceful and instead filled with excitement and raucous laughter.

The following day, Chris was invited to the second round of an English Speaking Contest. One of Mr Harrison's students spoke about True Love.

Speech

Jessica was very nervous and tripped on the way to the podium, but she managed to compose herself. She stood to take her turn:

'Good evening ladies, gentlemen and honourable judges:

What is true love? ... Each one of us will have a slightly different definition and even expectation of true love. Many people look for love in the man or woman of their dreams and a life full of romance and laughter. But is this true love? Or is it just a temporary experience? By the time it comes to the wedding day, perhaps that in itself is an indicator that they have found true love. Then when a child comes along, that true love can be shared with another.

But love is true only when it stands the test of time. It can be tested by troubled times and sickness. True love is truly challenged in the trials of life, and when all the money is gone!

Surely true love also extends beyond the family! It is shown by commitment to the needy in the world. We have heard of countless national disasters recently throughout the world; perhaps we should rename them 'INTERnational disasters'. Alongside these disasters, we have stories of Good Samaritans, governments and welfare services from all over sharing their love in many ways, both to individuals and to neighbouring countries, providing relief in the face of suffering. Sometimes the generous countries and individuals are going through difficulties of their own and need support too, but they take a risk and give. In an ideal world those givers should have no need to fear as they too are deserving of support in a crisis. But there is no guarantee they will receive help in their hour of need. Even so, they STILL take a risk and sacrifice time and money. This takes commitment.

So, what is true love? It is difficult to define, but whether it is a loving relationship or countries supporting one another, it always involves COMMITMENT. True love can be anything from butterflies in your stomach to painful sacrifice.

Love brings hope. Without love there is no hope, as there will be no one concerned for your welfare.

Love brings hope to the orphans and the disabled.
It brings forgiveness to those who fall.
It establishes strong ties and sound relationships.
Love builds trust.
Love brings hope to a dying world.

We cannot survive without love in this world where disasters increase day by day – earthquakes, drought, floods, famine, disease and war.

Do not respond to problems in anger and fear; take the hand of love, and hope will not forsake you.'

Chris was asked to say a few words about the talks and found his audience very receptive and attentive. After many excited conversations with the contestants, he said his final farewells to Mr. Harrison and the students with a promise to return to China one day. He travelled back to his hotel happy but exhausted, and set about planning his trip to Hunan.

*

Meanwhile, the victims of the cat attack prepared to leave the hospital, having been cleared of their worries about rabies.

"What made that cat do that? It went mad!" said Dad.

"I've no idea," replied Mum, "Perhaps it liked your aftershave!"

"It's not funny, it could have permanently damaged the nerve endings in my shoulder or passed on a deadly disease!"

"I know, I'm only kidding. But you're fine!"

"You don't realise how painful it is!"

"I know, I'm sorry. We'll look after you...what do you want to do? Do you want to go out somewhere or just go back home? Your choice."

"I don't know. How about visiting the Cathedral, since Michelle's going to have her awards ceremony there."

"Oh...okay," said Mum wishing she hadn't given him the choice.

Michelle took her Mum and Dad to Chester Cathedral, not divulging the fact that she intended not to go to her awards ceremony. Michelle was getting a bit bored in the end waiting for her parents to finish looking in the gift shop so she wandered back into the nave where the ceremony was going to take place in a few months' time. Funnily enough, her fiance Chris didn't really like ornate church buildings and cathedrals even though he was religious. She on the other hand could really appreciate the creativity in the architecture and the symbolism it held.

Michelle was still aching in her heart over Chris and couldn't wait for him to get back to England and to her! She was feeling anxious about the future. Just then, only just audible over some quiet chatter to her left, she heard someone speak. It was quite easily discernible even though it was a quiet voice. It said:

'One day, you will dance with the darkness of days. Finally you will rest in his arms and understand. Do not forsake the one at the right time. You will be faithful to the end.'

She looked round and couldn't see where it could have come from. The few people around her that the voice could have come from were either out of earshot or speaking quietly to each other. As she pondered over this and the content of what she heard, she heard it again in exactly the same way. She continued to look round and look up to the high ceiling. She even began to feel a slight sense of panic as she couldn't for the life of her work out where the voice was coming from. Then the words gently repeated themselves again, and for some reason she felt the voice was speaking to her.

In spite of being unnerved, she remained seated in the Cathedral and tried to understand the content of the message or advice the words conveyed. She thought to herself, 'Wouldn't it be amazing if it was a ghost or something telling me I am going to marry Chris,' but then she could only accept half the message, after all, what was the 'darkness of days' referring to? She resolutely decided to keep it all to herself, although she liked the bit that said, 'Finally you will rest in his arms.'

Michelle had no intention of ever telling anyone what she heard in the Cathedral as they would think she was mad. She wasn't ever going to tell Chris either! 'It was just my imagination,' she thought.

WATCHERS

Animals are feeling the heat. Their time of hiding in the wilds of the world is coming to an end; from elephants and tigers to mice and squirrels, from the fish of the sea, small and large, to the diverse birds of the air. The only safe places will be the cities, but the city dwellers will also be at risk. True love will be stretched too thin.

CHAPTER 6

Converging Plans

At the same point in time, plans were made independently and in their respective countries, plans that would bring about a meeting of opposing forces. It was 9:34am in Jamaica, and Joe and Edwina managed to book cheap flights to London for their family. They had always dreamed of seeing Tower Bridge, the Houses of Parliament and Big Ben situated in the Elizabeth Tower. Christaff was a bit young for the trip, but they were going to do it anyway and make use of their daughters' maternal skills to reduce the pressure. It was actually a promised business trip that Joe's boss demanded he fulfil. Once again, the Olivers were making the most of the opportunity.

It was 3:34pm in England and Michelle sat in the living room talking to Jinny and Frank who had an hour earlier arrived in Winchester to stay with them en route to France. Frank wasn't very communicative and had an expressionless face most of the time, looking 'spaced out'. Nevertheless, plans were finalised for their trip to Gatwick Airport.

Meanwhile, it was 10:34pm in Xi'an and Chris finally received a text to confirm the availability of a plane ticket to England. He lay on his hotel bed looking up at the ceiling, considering the contrast between his idyllic holiday in China, and the horror of the Glasgow and Russian earthquakes. He had earlier become aware of the accuracy of the Russian death toll figures. The news stated that it was not half a million as at first believed, but was in fact closer to a million! As he pondered the mysteries of life, he sent a text message to Michelle letting her know the exact time of his arrival in England the following week.

Chris had been enjoying his time in China so much he felt guilty somehow. 'So many people are suffering!' he thought. But he knew his holiday would soon come to an end and decided to make the most of it. He had heard about the beautiful mountain landscapes in Zhang Jia Jie in Hunan, so he had decided to spend a few days there just before he travelled back to England. Everything was arranged, so after he had sent the text, he packed his bags for the trip.

Train to Zhang Jia Jie

He had already heard the reputation the green trains had in China. Even so, he was not prepared for what hit him. He boarded the train and the floor was caked in dirt and litter. He had been allocated one of the beds at the top of the three tiered bunk beds called hard sleepers. There were six beds in each open compartment. Chris had to have the pillow replaced as it had shoe prints all over the surface. While it was still early evening he sat on a small seat in the corridor next to a tiny table that had not been cleaned for years. The carriage floor was covered in squashed-in old food with brown stains almost completely hiding the original turquoise coloured lino. To his surprise the Chinese passengers did not look at all concerned about any of it. Chris felt a bit embarrassed as he could tell the other passengers noticed his distress. The train set off and was moving very slowly. In the middle of the night it was far too hot for him to sleep in his bed. One thing that did not help was the fact that the compartment fan was not working properly. The young teenage boy in the bunk directly opposite him was also struggling to sleep in the heat and kept yelping to his Mum, but he found a way to get the fan working for short bursts by manoeuvring it into various positions with his foot. The problem was, it only blew on him and none of the other five passengers in the compartment. This proved difficult for the boy too as his leg kept getting tired. At about 11pm, the boy's travelling friend joined him in his bed and they took turns to position the precarious fan with their feet. Chris was worried in case the broken fan sent an electric shock through the boy's body. Every fifteen minutes or so, Chris would hear the words 'lao wai' and then for two or three minutes feel an intermittent draught of cool air helping him to breathe again in the unbearable heat as they kindly aimed the fan at him.

After midnight, the fan had completely gone to sleep, along with his five compartment companions. Every time Chris began to drop off to sleep he would wake up gasping for air. This, coupled with his concern over the squash and the dirt, meant he had to contort his body again to climb down from his bunk and sit on the little seat in the corridor in the dark, even though he was extremely tired. This was the beginning of an awesome experience.

The windows were lifted up to the halfway position and the curtains tied back. The wind blew with such force into the carriage that the temperature just next to the window was perfect. In the process, Chris' T-shirt violently flapped and wriggled along with the tied back curtains. It was like a dream. He had a clear view out of the train window. He felt like he was one with the dark landscape. The land outside was mysterious and misty under a bright half-moon. The Moon was positioned at an angle in such a way that it appeared to be smiling. As the curtains continued to flap in the wind along with his T-shirt, it somehow felt like nothing in the world mattered.

Although he couldn't explain why, this was one of the most profound experiences he had ever had. He had gone from terrible discomfort to a heavenly experience that did not even take into consideration his discomfort. He had such a mysterious awareness of God's authority and power. God could do anything and create everything! It was a very spiritual experience, and he couldn't help the tears filling his eyes.

A lady with a pink baggy 'party dress' sat on one of the small seats at the far end of the carriage in the darkness with her little child. This reminded Chris he was part of the human race and all the responsibilities that that involved. He was convinced this beautiful experience would not have 'reached' him if he had not been so uncomfortable before. It made him aware of just how much God is in control in spite of the appearance of chaos in today's world. Suffering is an inevitable part of life, but it can lead to a greater revelation of the miracle of life.

The Mountains

This was not his only moving experience. After settling into Zhang Jia Jie he enjoyed the magnificent views from Tian Men Mountain and the peaceful serenity of Bao Feng Lake.

One day, Chris looked upon the 'Alleluia Mountains' from the Tian Zi area and it simply reinforced his sense of awe at the wonders of creation. He stood on one of the viewing platforms reached only by road. Very few holidaymakers ventured that far, so he was able to view it in solitude. Tears began to fill his eyes again, blurring the beauty of the vast scene, but it was not a scene he could easily forget.

When the time came for him to travel back to Xi'an, it was again a long and uncomfortable journey, but this time he was equipped with a collection of breath-taking memories.

*

In contrast to this beauty, in Jamaica baby Christaff was already having an oppressive influence on his family. They were going to be very important to his future and the baby needed a stable environment in which to grow and learn to ensure his success. It was as if his family were in a big invisible bubble. The more he could keep them all around him the better!

Rumblings

There was an expectancy in the air as the east coast of England was expecting a battering from a huge hurricane. No one knew for certain where the hurricane would strike, but all along the coast people had boarded up their windows and put their precious plants into sheds and garages.

People stood in their anoraks and woolly jumpers, feeling an unusual chill in the atmosphere. The grey sky came with a clammy moisture. Many in large detached houses glared towards the sea out of their big study windows feeling both anxious and secure. Dark clouds loomed across the whole eastern horizon and the English could sense the boding winds like a brooding chorus from a thousand distant voices clinging to their ears.

But secretly, slowly and stealthily, the hurricane meandered northward.

Reflection

Having returned from his wonderful trip to Hunan, Chris sat on a rock at Xi'an's Qujiang Park, looking at the calm pool in the twilight. As usual there was no breeze brushing against the reeds. Everything was still and calm, ideal for contemplation. He contemplated his future. He thought about his experiences and what they told him about his values in life.

50

He threw some bread into the water as he got up because he noticed a couple of small fish swimming close by. He started to move away from the water and head for the path. Chris thought he could hear a sudden rushing of water and at the back of his mind he thought it was just a surge of water coming over the rocks further up the pool. Actually, it was a school of fish fighting and scrambling for the tasty snack as though their lives depended on it.

This was his last visit to his favourite park before his return flight to England.

WATCHERS

Such beauty and ugliness, side by side! We cannot remove all hope or no one will emerge intact. There may be years ahead with no sign of deliverance so let's watch carefully to ensure the chosen ones endure to the end.

CHAPTER 7

Power Clash

Christaff sat on Edwina's knee on the London-bound plane and fell into a trance-like state. He had a dream of himself, a baby, sitting on an altar in the Jewish temple in Israel. In his vision, he was smiling, and feeling great excitement. He saw solemn faced representatives of every nation in the world bowing before him with their heads to the ground. The only problem was, there was actually no temple in Jerusalem or indeed anywhere in Israel.

Simultaneously, Edwina spoke about returning to Israel one day and trying to be the Jew she thought she should be, but subconsciously they were both trying to somehow find a way to make up for the terrible mistake they had made with Mamosa's friend.

Christaff and his parents flew towards Heathrow airport as Jinny and Frank took off from Gatwick on their plane to France. As the two planes crossed paths, the turbulence surprised even the pilots.

Michelle and her parents had seen off Frank and Jinny, and then travelled to Heathrow to await Chris' return from China.

*

Chris and Michelle were overjoyed to see one another, but Michelle's parents were there all the time so they were more reserved than they wanted to be.

As they all entered London city, they could see the London Eye slowly turning, itself looking down upon the people of London city.

Through the London streets they witnessed lots of arguments. For example, on Oxford Street they saw a man repeatedly punching a woman of a similar age in her face, with no sense of hesitation or restraint. Just as they were wondering what to do to help, they were relieved to see a couple of policemen running to the scene of the crime. A little later, they saw a car driver deliberately speed up his car near a Pelican crossing and run straight into a couple of young men. People attended to them and an ambulance was called. This was not to mention the arguments and the screaming between mums and their young children. This was certainly unusual. These

53

things happened everywhere in the world, but not this frequently in one place. Something strange was happening to people. They had no patience! Michelle's Dad and Chris discussed the social problems that a big British city like London had, but they couldn't remember it ever being that bad on previous visits. They had to assume it was just coincidence, because there was no logical reason they could think of that would explain the phenomena.

Chris and Michelle held hands wishing they could hold each other tight, but they couldn't in public as they hadn't shared about 'their decision' as Chris would put it. For all they knew, either one of them could have decided not to get married, even if they still had feelings for one another. The awkwardness would be just too much in front of other people, so they hesitated.

Michelle was overjoyed to be with Chris, but was constantly on edge as they needed time together to talk. She tried to think how they could be alone long enough for Chris to tell her his feelings. It was so frustrating! Eventually, Michelle came up with a plan. She lied and told her Mum she still needed to buy her another belated birthday present and Chris had promised to help her when he got back. Mum felt touched by this and didn't hesitate saying, "Oh thank you, of course, you two go off and take the opportunity to catch up while you're at it."

"Thanks Mum," said Michelle. They all arranged a rendezvous point for meeting up later, and Chris and Michelle dashed off together hand in hand.

They were so distracted by each other that Chris bumped into a buggy being pushed by the baby's mother. "Oh, I'm really sorry!" said Chris. "Don't worry," said Mama, "You are obviously too in love to notice what's happening around you." Michelle and Chris hadn't had their chat yet, so couldn't say "Yes we are!" So instead they just smiled.

Just then, Chris' eyes met the baby's. Chris felt his heart pounding as though he was suffering some kind of shock. Somehow, seeing the baby disturbed him but he didn't know why. He couldn't see anything physically strange about the baby. Chris stood back hesitantly while Michelle tickled the baby under his chin. "What's your baby called?" asked Michelle. "Christaff, Christaff Young," answered its Mama as the baby gripped Michelle's index finger tightly, as though he was familiar with her.

She noticed Chris was a bit distant, so she carefully prised her fingers from the baby's surprisingly large hand and said goodbye. Will they ever meet Christaff again? What are the chances?

Noticing Chris step back reticently, Joe was wondering why people were not cooing at their baby as much as they do with other people's babies. Since Christaff was born, Edwina and Joe were on the road to becoming emotional recluses. They did however remain extremely close to each other which gave stability to the baby. Even Joe's daughters were becoming increasingly obsessively loyal to the nuclear family. Unbeknown to them the whole family was becoming less individualistic; their minds were becoming pliable to invisible forces.

*

Chris and Michelle eventually got their alone-time. Instead of shopping like Michelle said, they quickly found a cafe so they could have a chat. They found a quiet corner and sat down with their coffee, both looking at each other, tearful and expectant.

WATCHERS

Soon the stirring and tossing of the seas will start. This will give them a sense of the awesome power of Creation. They will feel totally out of control and cry for help. Let's hope they cry to the one who can help them. But first, things must continue to take their course. Meanwhile, the Beast touches many and leaves a stain wherever he goes.

Part 3

BLUE MURDER

CHAPTER 8

The Nutty Professor

George, a stereotypical 'nutty professor' lookalike, wasn't the slightest bit interested in Maths, Physics or Chemistry. He had however always been an avid reader. Now he was retired he was a loyal and very mature student at the weekly Leeds Readers' Association meetings. It kept his brain ticking over and gave him a regular retirement pursuit to occupy himself with. He enjoyed going through the preparatory work before the next class, and actually seemed to put more effort into his homework than anyone else. His English Literature classes were really leaving a lasting impression on him; *twas brillig*, or so he thought.

After the class he packed his briefcase with 'Through The Looking Glass, And What Alice Found There' along with the accompanying class notes. He admired the style of Lewis Carroll's 'literary nonsense'.

The metal object's razor sharp edge twinkled.
"Snicker-snack! Snicker-snack!" it whispered.

Stepping out into the Autumn evening, sidestepping the muddy fallen leaves, he strode down the *tulgey* street. A misty haze shrouded his mind's eye above his forehead bringing with it a headache. Although he found it hard to focus his thoughts he could picture his fellow students sat in the classroom. He liked his class-mates … 'although some are *slithy toves,* especially the one in the striped T-shirt!' He couldn't shake off an image of a fellow student talking and talking and talking … 'and dominating the WHOLE CLASS! *The jaws that bite, the claws that catch! Beware the Jubjub bird!*' George's right hand twitched and tried to clench itself tight.

The stainless steel object of death spoke again,
growing impatient, vibrating in expectation.
"Snicker-snack! Snicker-snack!" it called.
"Beware the Jabberwock, my son!"

'Then there's that sleazy young man, thinking he's the teacher's pet, trying to get ALL the attention, *THE FRUMIOUS BANDERSNATCH!*'

"Snicker-snack! Snicker-snack!" throbbed the lonesome
object, the metal blade now feeling assured.
On the table it lay, reclining and waiting for its fun.
"Snicker-snack! Snicker-snack!" it whispered
faster and more...
"Snicker-snack! Snicker-snack!"

'I like my literature class, I've learnt so much and become ... I hate those smug intellectuals who think they own the world!' Suddenly, all went calm as he inserted his key into the lock of his front door. The handle turned, the familiar voice of his wife rang out from the kitchen ... and a whisper met his ears:

"Take me, use me, I will release you. *Snicker-snack!*
Snicker-snack! Snicker-snack! Snicker-snack!"

He managed to ignore the whispers and hunched his shoulders. Something was on his back, invisible but heavy...

"Take me, use me, I will release you. *Snicker-snack!"*

Entering the dining room *he took his vorpal sword in hand.* It spoke to him. That moment his wife *came whiffling* into the room. He *stood awhile in thought.* Having picked up the tool of release and *with eyes aflame: One, two! One, two! And through and through the vorpal blade went snicker-snack! Snicker-snack! Snicker-snack! Snicker-snack! Snicker-snack! Snicker-snack! Snicker-snack! He left it dead ... with its head* hanging *back* ......

"And hast thou slain the Jabberwock?
Come to my arms my beamish boy!
O frabjous day! Callooh! Callay!"

Twas brillig, and the slithy toves ceased
*gyr*ing *and gimbl*ing *in the wabe.*

And now, at last, *all mimsy were the borogoves,*
And no longer feared he if *the mome raths outgrabe*d.

In *uffish thought* he trudged with short hunched steps
into the living room,
so rested he by the Tumtum tree.

Meanwhile, lifeless around the floor she lay
in the dining room,
Raw flesh razored, sliced and diced for all to see.
O frabjous day!
O frabjous day!

Timeless and motionless rested he
in no man's land free
this was meant to be
he and only he
all else is history
'No more for me!'
"What's for tea?"
Can't they see?
"Sorry!"
'See.'

The Police

Sergeant Mandible and Detective Inspector Riddly didn't know how long the suspect had been sat staring at the blank television screen. He was completely unresponsive and just kept glaring into the TV. Forensic scientists placed markers against the body parts and took photos.

"What's your name, sir? Are you Dr. George Mason?" Mandible asked. "Sir! Sir! SIR!"

"We're going to have to ask you to come down to the police station to answer a few questions, alright sir? Is there anyone we can call for you? Mr. Mason ... Mr. Mason ..." said PC Venture attempting a feminine touch. It was no use, George was beyond help at that moment.

This wasn't the first case like it in the reasonably quiet suburb.

There had already been five similar murders there in the last two months. They were all equally unexplainable. George had no criminal record and had an impeccable employment record.

These events were not only confined to Leeds. Actually, throughout the world murder and domestic violence were on the increase. Theories were being considered in regard to this and scientists were seeing if there was perhaps a link with the increased global attacks on humans from wild animals, such as the unprecedented increase in deaths from attacks by bears and wolves in Canada.

"Come with us sir ... that's it ... watch your step ... okay?"

George trudged slowly with his head down. He glanced over to his wife's body as they passed through the dining room on the way to the back door. "What's for tea Maggie?" he uttered with a mellow croak.

WATCHERS

They cannot contain all these offenders in the prisons. There is no room. They will resort to leniency, and in some places a greater amount receiving the death penalty. Morals will be challenged and become even more unfashionable.

CHAPTER 9

Daydreaming Teacher

"Good morning boys and girls!"

"Good morning Mr. Carter, good morning everyone!" replied the children sat on the carpet round the teacher's reading chair.

"Now then, Michael, what is the weather like today?" asked Chris, their teacher.

"Rainy."

"Yes, that's right, and ....?" he asked gently, expecting Michael to elaborate.

"Wet!" said Michael, proud of himself.

"Yes, it usually is wet when it's raining."

"Very very VERY rainy," added Jessica.

"Yes, it's very rainy but not very very rainy. But, what else is it doing outside?"

Graham knelt up and peered out of the window, "Some children are coming to school!"

"Oh!" said Chris, "Who is late for school I wonder?"

Unfortunately, the children took this as a cue to get up and move over to the window.

"No! Sit down! Sit down!" exclaimed their teacher getting quite frustrated now.

"So, who is going to answer my question about the weather?"

"I ... I ... I ... went to ... I went to see my auntie on Sunday ..."

"That's very interesting Taniel, but ..."

" ... and ... and ... and it was rainy!"

"Oh very good."

"And ... and ... and ..."

Chris interrupted, "It's raining outside, but it's not only raining is it? It's ...?"

"It's stopped raining!" shouted Isabella.

All the children started to leave the carpet again and head for the window. Just then there was a knock on the classroom door and in walked the Head Teacher.

"Sit down children!" Chris said in a panic trying to think of an excuse for the chaos. "We will explore the colours outside later ... and look! We have a special visitor!"

"Good morning Mr. Carter, good morning children."

"Good morning Mr. Bywater, good morning everyone," said the class.

"No, you don't have to say 'everyone' again, you've al..."

"That's okay Mr. Carter," said the Head Teacher reassuringly. "I thought I would just let you know that one of Her Majesty's Inspectors is coming into school today. Enjoy your lesson," said Mr. Bywater, who smiled to himself on the way out.

'I can't believe it!' screamed Chris in his head. 'Why are we having an Inspector in the school? How can I concentrate on teaching now? He could have told me before!'

"Mr. Carter, what is the weather doing now?" asked Chantelle, being the model pupil.

"Oh … windy! Get your reading books out please." The children collected their reading books and eventually settled into their seats after ten minutes of clattering and banging. Mrs. Rose the teaching assistant arrived and sat with the lower ability group while Chris sat behind his teacher's desk sweating. He hoped Mrs. Rose could discern his 'real' reason for not interacting with the children. He was obviously giving the children an opportunity to use their independent learning skills, while he 'confidently' checked his lesson plans were up to scratch. 'If the Inspector sees these he'll do his nut!' he thought.

After ten minutes of checking and rechecking his plans, his tired mind began to drift. He reminisced over his decision whether or not to marry Michelle, thinking back to the conversation he had with her the day he got back from China:

In the cafe, they looked deeply into each other's eyes and Michelle thought, 'Surely, by the way I feel and by the way he's looking at me, he can't have decided to call it off.'

"So, you don't want to marry me then?" ventured Michelle.

"What do you think?" said Chris keeping her in suspense.

"Well I don't believe in God, so … all I know is I love you and I think you love me … it's simple. You either want me or you don't. And if you can't decide now, then we'd better call it all off!"

Michelle looked down pouting slightly.

"Well … er … yes."

"What! Yes what?"

"I mean yes I want to marry you," answered Chris.

"You need to be clearer! You may want to marry me, but you have not said you WILL marry me!"

"Well ... er ..."

That was just too much. Michelle got up, leant over the table and grabbed Chris by the scruff of his neck.

Chris laughed and said, "Alright alright I'll marry you."

"Stop joking with me and tell me the truth!"

"I'm sorry, I know, I'm being horrible."

"You are! You've been away for four weeks enjoying yourself and I've been stuck here with my Mum and Dad moaning at each other, not knowing whether my life is going to be turned upside down or not ... you are so mean," she said slapping him on his arm.

"I do want to mar ... er I WILL marry you. Of course I will. I can't imagine life without you," said Chris putting her out of her misery.

"So you've no problem with me not believing in God then? So I don't need to worry about you changing your mind again?" asked Michelle making sure.

"I have definitely decided to marry you, but I still think it may cause problems."

"We've talked about all this before," said Michelle not wanting to go over old ground again.

"I know but it is important."

"I know, but I can't believe in something I don't believe in!"

"Perhaps you just don't want to believe!" snapped Chris.

Michelle got up from the table crying ... Chris rushed to her side and put his arm round her saying, "Look, I'm not saying it's always going to be easy, but we love each other and we're going to get married. Isn't that enough?"

Michelle just looked down with tears in her eyes. "Are you sure you are not going to change your mind again?"

"Yes I'm sure, and I never did change my mind, I just needed to think things through. Come and sit down." They sat side by side holding each other tight not caring about everyone in the cafe staring at them. They talked about everything that had happened in China and England over the last four weeks. It felt like time had stood still and they didn't realise it was getting late.

After their second coffee, they prepared to leave, and Chris *finally plucked up courage to pull the little box from his pocket. He took out the diamond engagement ring. Michelle was fiddling in her handbag for something. "Michelle ..." he said.*

"What," she replied casually, still fumbling in her bag.

"Will you marry me?"

"Yes of course." Then she realised he was speaking formally. "Oh ... oh, yes."

Chris took hold of her left hand and attempted to gently place the ring on her finger. It was too tight, but he tried anyway.

"Oh that's beautiful, thank you, oh how romantic!"

Chris felt really uncomfortable in public, especially as several people on the tables next to them buried their faces in their hands giggling. He was also worried in case the diamond was a fake and Michelle would be able to tell. But surely it was the real thing. He loved her so much and was absolutely over the moon, but at the back of his mind he buried a sense of guilt at not marrying a Christian.

"Thank you Chris. I don't want to lose you. When shall we make the announcement?"

"Whenever you like."

They left the cafe arm in arm. The future looked bright and nothing else mattered at that moment.

"Mr. Carter ... Mr. Carter ... Mr. Carter!"

"Yes ... oh hi, er hello, er good evening ... no ..." Chris realised he had completely blown it. He quickly gave a formal cough and stood to attention. Sounding professional he said, "Good morning, I'm Chris Carter." He shook hands with the Inspector and accidentally did the same with the Headmaster.

"Mr. Carter is working with this class only once a week; the rest of the time, he teaches in Key Stage 2, but we thought this would be good for his professional development since he's a new teacher," said the Headmaster.

"And how do you like teaching in Key Stage 1 Mr. Carter?" asked the Inspector.

Chris had to choose his words carefully. He thought, 'The Inspector is a woman so she likes little children, she might be a mother even though she's dressed like a man, she looks like she has a sensitive side so I need to show a glint of sensitivity in my 'professional' response ...' He formulated all of this in a micro-second: "Er ... good." He just couldn't get the words out!

"Are these your lesson plans?"

"Er ... yes."

"Mm ... I see you've differentiated for each ability group."

"Yes ..."

"Do you have any 'statements'?"

"No," replied Chris trying to sound definite, assertive and professional.

"They look very good, thank you Mr. Carter."

"Thank you, thank you ..." He had to stop himself from going over the top. The Head and the Inspector left the classroom.

'I can't believe it, she liked my lesson plans,' Chris thought, flopping back into his chair behind his desk. He then realised he had had a very lucky escape. He did have a child with a 'statement', he had Luke with Autism! Phew! Then he pictured his next meeting with the Head who must have noticed his mistake.

*

Meanwhile, anoraks and woolly jumpers could be seen floating through the mire masking the roads of Norfolk and Suffolk. The clothing contained the bodies of those who were unprepared. Many had still been in the process of boarding up their windows for a second time to protect their homes from wind and sea. The Meteorological Society had not managed to get out accurate information in time. Hurricane Gordon had fooled them all. A hundred died and hundreds were missing as the sea claimed the eastern coast.

*

"How did your week at work go?" asked Michelle.

"Oh, wonderful!"

"Really?"

"What do you think?"

"I guess not!"

"We had an Inspector in. The only warning I got was the Head walking in on my lesson the same morning just while the children were clambering all over the place!" exclaimed Chris sulking. "I wouldn't mind, but she wasn't even actually inspecting anything, she's just the Head's friend. It didn't stop her checking my lesson plans though!"

"Don't worry, the Head's just keeping you on your toes, that's all."

"He hates me, I know he does."

"Don't be daft, he's only just employed you and you're a new teacher."

"I'm never going to pass my first year."

"Come here!" She gave him a big kiss.

*

The news was on TV in the living room while Michelle made some blueberry and raspberry smoothies:

'Great Britain has witnessed yet another unprecedented disaster ....'

"Look at this, Shell!"

"What is it?"

"It's showing you pictures of the hurricane disaster."

"I know, I've seen them."

"Don't you think it's strange, all this stuff that's happening?"

"What do you mean?"

"You know. All the big disasters. I think it's a sign of some sort."

"Oh, here we go!"

"I'm just saying, I think it's a message ..."

"Here's your smoothie!"

"Thanks," said Chris taking a slurp.

"Look, it's the weekend. I'm as upset about it as you but we are here and they are there. We can't do anything about it, so relax; you need to unwind otherwise you'll be too tired to drive back to Berkshire on Sunday night. Mum and Dad have gone out so we can spend some time together."

"Okay."

"Mum and Dad don't like our wedding guest list by the way!"

70

"Hey! We're supposed to be relaxing, remember?"

"Don't you care about the wedding?"

"Of course I do!"

"And ... there's another problem."

"What?"

"The Vicar can't do a winter wedding."

"It just gets better and better!"

"Well, he said he would let us know for sure in a couple of weeks."

"I'll phone him later and let him know how much we want one. If we leave it until March there's going to be no England left."

WATCHERS

Little by little the tide will turn,
The faithful will come and the chaff will burn.
Footstep by footstep the army will rise,
To sweep away evil, let goodness surprise.

So lift up your heads,
Your deliverance is nigh.
Abandon corruption
And take to the sky.

CHAPTER 10

Hitched

The annual tidal bore was due on the Qian Tang River in Zhejiang Province, but the previous year had been a bit of a disappointment in comparison to other years, so the residents alongside the River were not sufficiently protected from what was to come. No one had predicted the changes that were taking place in the Moon's orbit and its closer proximity to the Earth.

Evacuation procedures were in place and most had followed instructions. However, there remained hundreds of residents who decided to sit it out. People's possessions were for the most part left in their homes as evacuation would have been very difficult if everyone transported all their household items and furniture. Nevertheless, the waves were so high that the barriers were completely swamped, and the water ceaselessly claimed land and housing. Many evacuees were also killed as their rescue stations were too close. Yet the Moon just rested above them, majestically looking upon the slaughter.

As a result, scientists started to issue early warnings about the next proxigean spring tide and its possible effect upon various parts of the world.

From country to country and region to region, the human race was trying to come to terms with all the international disasters. Subconsciously they were beginning to try to find something to cling to, to depend on. Some turned to God and others turned to the pursuit of wealth and greed.

*

"Hey Shell! It's okay to have a late winter wedding, the Vicar has made our alternative February date official. I sent a message to Wang Bin as well to see if he could still come. He's going to be touring the UK for his whole winter holiday, so he'll still have time to come before he goes back to China. Zhang Lili said she can't come for some reason," said Chris.

"Okay, so we can make proper arrangements now," replied Michelle.

Zhang Lili visited Xi'an's Qujiang Park and remembered something Chris had said to her: "We'll weather the weather whatever the weather". He had used this to illustrate his belief that the British would get through the terrible occurrences in his country. She tried to apply this saying to herself, because she was so disappointed about missing the trip to England. She desperately wanted to meet more English people like Chris, but she didn't have the money to go with Wang Bin, and her parents insisted she kept her promise to do some work experience they had arranged for the winter holiday, not to mention their expectations in regard to celebrating the Chinese New Year with her family. But, when would she ever get a chance like this again? How often would she get an invitation to England? Chris was her sole contact in the UK! It would have been a dream come true to attend a traditional English white wedding. She would just make sure she kept in regular contact with Chris and his wife in the future.

As she walked alongside South Lake at the park, she could hear frequent deep gurgling sounds coming from the water. She could also see occasional disturbances in the Lake, and periodic clusters of large bubbles rising to the surface. She guessed it was just the season for overactive fish, but then Zhang Lili heard a tremendous crashing sound combined with the sound of rushing; it was deafening! As she attempted to comprehend what was going on, she heard a crescendo of men and women's screams. Zhang Lili looked around to see what was going on. She noticed people's faces looking towards the Lake. Her eyes focused on what was once a majestic stretch of water, and saw a deep empty bowl shape at the bottom of which were pockets of people crawling around in mud, and peddle boats dotted around them. Covering the whole base of what was the South Lake were many thousands of fish and fresh water creatures wriggling in piles as they pined for their watery home.

At that moment there was an intensifying shaking as the earth stretched and imbibed the drink. This tremor made little further change to the landscape, but it did put the stranded creatures in further distress as fish disappeared below the surface of the Lake bed, along with most of the surviving boaters.

*

Michelle was out with Chris, and as usual, her Dad was glued to the telly at home. Mum was bringing in his supper as the news was being broadcast:

'The disease outbreak is believed to be Cholera. There are three reported cases from Norfolk. The patients are being treated in the Norfolk and Norwich Hospital while twenty others are isolated for tests. The residents of Norfolk and Suffolk have been advised to stay in their locality and to only drink water provided by the council.

'Famine and disease is continuing to escalate throughout the world, the worst hit being Africa ...'

"Oh, are you really sure you want to watch this darling?"
"Yes, we need to know what's happening in the world. There's probably going to be an outbreak of Cholera. Did you know its nickname is The Blue Death?"
"No I didn't."
"Its called The Blue Death because that's the colour you go when you're about to die!"
"Right! That's it! It's going off!" she exclaimed grabbing the controls. He grabbed the controls back and scratched her hand badly with his finger nails in the process. Screaming blue murder, she ran to the kitchen sink to wash the blood off her hand. Dad continued to watch the telly:

'Residents are being asked to be vigilant and seek medical help if they are suffering from extreme diarrhea and vomiting.'

Michelle's Mum could hear the news from the kitchen and scrubbed her hand too hard in her distress.

'News is coming in of an earthquake in Los Angeles ...'

Hearing this last statement was just too much for her to bear.

75

With her hands still wet she rushed into the living room, grabbed the TV in both hands, ripped it from the wall and smashed it onto the floor. Sparks flashed from the TV set.

In blind fury, Michelle's Dad got up out of his seat and punched his wife in the stomach. Like a statue he looked down on her as she crumpled up on the floor breathless. He couldn't move or even utter a response to the distress his wife was displaying. He couldn't believe what he had done. Smoke rose from the broken TV set as Michelle's Mum began to wheeze trying to catch her breath. "Mary, I'm sorry. Mary! Mary!" He felt like the world had ended. 'How could things get so bad?' he thought.

Four Months Passed

The Wedding

The organist played The Bridal March and Michelle and her Dad walked down All Saints' Church aisle together, followed by five beautiful bridesmaids dressed in delicate silky blue and carrying bright colourful flowers. Just behind the Bride were Chris' older and younger sisters. The three very young bridesmaids were Michelle's cousins. Everybody gazed admiringly at Michelle in her majestic white dress, her face covered by a veil as she was slowly accompanied between the walls of delicate lilac and blue flower arrangements at the edges of the pews. She tried to ignore the eyes and focus ahead at Chris in his smart black suit stood near his Best Man. The Bride sidled beside her future husband and the two older bridesmaids excitedly yet reverently lifted the bridal veil, savouring the awesome moment.

The Vicar took his position at the front of the church:

"A warm welcome to everyone on this special occasion: the marriage of Christopher and Michelle."

After a few words of introduction, he asked:

"Who gives this woman to be married to this man?"

Michelle's Dad placed his daughter's hand into the Vicar's and the

Vicar gave her hand to Chris, who looked into her eyes and said:

"I Chris take you Michelle to be my wife, to have and to hold from this day forward. For better for worse, for richer for poorer, in sickness and in health, to love and to cherish, till death us do part, according to God's holy law. In the presence of God I make this vow."

Michelle then took Chris' hand and recited the same vow. Then the rings were produced. The Vicar prayed:

"Heavenly Father, let these rings be to Michelle and Chris a symbol of unending love and faithfulness, to remind them of the vow and covenant which they have made this day. Through Jesus Christ our Lord. Amen."

Chris placed the ring on Michelle's finger first and then recited the following:

"I give you this ring as a sign of our marriage. With my body I honour you. All that I am I give to you. All that I have I share with you, within the love of God, the Father, Son and Holy Spirit."

Michelle did the same. The Vicar then declared:

"Those whom God has joined together let no one put asunder."

Then, looking at the newlyweds, he said:

"You may now kiss the Bride."

Everyone cheered as Chris planted one on Michelle. Guests in the congregation fiddled with their boxes of confetti. Even though the church had asked them to refrain from throwing confetti in the church grounds, there had been a rebellious conspiracy amongst Michelle's friends - no way were they going to miss this opportunity!

*

Everyone finally arrived at the hotel for the Reception. When the Bride and Groom got there they were still caked in multicoloured confetti. The guests were starving, and from time to time sneaked into the Banquet Hall to check the seating arrangements. Eventually, the meal was officially started and they had their fill of food and wine.

Afterwards, Michelle's Dad stood to make the first speech:

"Michelle is the apple of my eye. She may not know it, but it's true. When she first introduced us to Chris I thought, 'What on earth have we got here! Poor Michelle!'"

People politely laughed.

"But I have found Chris to be a decent, intelligent young man who knows what he wants out of life and he knows he wants to spend the rest of his life with my daughter, and that's good enough for me. As the saying goes, I won't be losing a daughter, I'll be gaining a son. And I want to say to Chris and to Michelle, we will always be there for you, if you ever need advice or you just want to visit. And please ... don't forget your old Dad!"

Michelle was touched by her Dad's words but she knew she would never ask him for advice. But then she began to feel a sense of guilt as she looked up at him speaking affectionately about her. She actually longed for her Dad to love her just as she was. But why did she think he didn't? She tried to rationalise her bad feelings towards her Dad, how he had let her down, such as not staying overnight in Chester when she was at university. But, hang on! Mum didn't stay either and she was not angry with her! She frantically tried to think of all the reasons why she didn't respect her Dad as a daughter should. Her emotions were racing through her mind and heart almost uncontrollably, but she couldn't for the life of her think of anything to justify her attitude towards her Dad. The most she could do was identify his character flaws, but then everybody had those in one way or another. She felt sorry for the way she had treated her Dad all her life.

Dad continued with his well prepared and practiced speech:

"I am so proud of my little girl. She is now a beautiful and sophisticated young woman but she will always be my special little girl."

That was too much for Michelle to cope with; she started to cry and her make-up began to run. Chris could put his arm round her but was useless with make-up, so the chief bridesmaid scurried to the rescue.

Dad was a bit dumbfounded and was worried in case he had offended her, but then reasoned she must have been touched by his words. He felt everyone was expecting him to continue, so he endeavoured to do so. But then it hit him too. To his knowledge, Michelle had never been drawn to tears by touching words uttered by him. In fact he had barely ever expressed his affection for her in the past. It was because she had always been so stubborn and obnoxious! But was that any excuse? He resolved in his mind to change things. He was going to stop being such a bitter, emotionless and boring idiot. What must his wife think of him? She didn't want to be married to a man like him! Yet she always carried on being a faithful and committed wife! Things were going to change from now on!

Dad finished his speech with a heartfelt toast:

"Let's all stand together to toast the Bride and Groom. To the Bride and Groom!"

The guests rose from their comfy chairs and shouted, "To the Bride and Groom!"

Chris took his turn to speak to the guests and afterwards offered a toast to the five bridesmaids. The Best Man followed on but was so nervous he couldn't avoid stammering through his own jokes. After the toast he shouted, "Farewell to freedom, hello to the pattering of little feet!" He said this referring back to an occasion when he and Chris had discussed how many children they would have when they got married in the future.

After the speeches, Michelle's Dad just had to give his daughter a hug whether it fitted in with the proceedings or not. They held each other for ten minutes, saying how proud they were of each other, and as a consequence, ten years of hurt and unforgiveness were healed. Michelle's make-up began to run again!

The Chunnel

Amongst those leaving from the Cheriton terminal was Burt Jonson, looking forward to his long awaited trip to Calais and Paris. He had witnessed a slight earth tremor just before he boarded the passenger train, but he didn't concern himself too much about it. After all, he wouldn't be in England soon. At the start of the 50km underwater journey, along with many other passengers, he looked through the train window to see the Folkestone White Horse trembling as they departed from England. Burt got out his newspaper and settled back into his seat.

Kent trembled and quaked, and the White Cliffs of Dover shed a few layers. It was an underwater earthquake striking off the Kent coast and at that moment cracking the structure of the Channel Tunnel.

Water cascaded into the tunnel and everything went pitch black. Cars and trains dashed to and fro having no place to go, powered by the sea waters invading the tunnel. Burt and countless other people were as insignificant as ants being washed down a plug-hole.

*

When Jinny and Frank heard the news about the Chunnel disaster from French locals, they couldn't believe it. They had only just got back from attending Michelle and Chris' wedding, having travelled through the same tunnel! What was happening to the world? It could just as easily have happened to them!

Although they were living in a beautiful and quiet part of France, they were clearly not able to escape all the escalating disasters. The Chunnel disaster was not the only thing effecting France. In the village next to them there was a lot of attention being given to three people suffering a rare type of disease, or so they had heard. The villagers were from different families yet they must have caught the same disease simultaneously.

Some people were saying it was some sort of chemical leak, poisonous gases having been transported by the wind and deposited in the village of Fleur.

People from the surrounding villages were frantically trying to find out as much information as possible so they could protect themselves, or even move to another place until it had all been identified and treated. They saw ambulances frequently pass their villa and return the same way. Jinny and Frank didn't understand why French TV wasn't taking an interest in the story.

*

Meanwhile, Chris raised his glass towards Michelle in their Honeymoon Paradise hotel restaurant.

"Congratulations!" he said.

"What for?" responded Michelle.

"New beginnings."

"To new beginnings!"

"To new beginnings!"

"Cheers!"

"Cheers!"

WATCHERS

The Dragon is crafty and determined although he will never win; the wedding feast will be luxurious. However, the wedding guests must be ready.

The Bridegroom will come unexpectedly to claim his Bride, so everything has to be prepared according to plan. Those who try to spoil the celebration must be punished first. The worst and the best are still to come!

Part 4

A CHRISTMAS CRACKER

CHAPTER 11

Cult

'It is believed that the strange behaviour of animals throughout the world has some connection with the extreme seismic activity that has been affecting every continent with such regularity over the last few years. Any connection with disease has been ruled out. Scientists suggest there is also a link to magnetic forces. Magnetic forces in the atmosphere influence the way birds and animals behave or travel. Recently, the Earth's axis has undergone a significant shift and there has been an increase in solar flare activity. It is thought these things may also have an influence upon the behaviour of wildlife. Later on in the programme, we are going to hand over to John Martin our reporter in Washington where experiments have been carried out to find answers to these worldwide phenomena. Meanwhile, religious fundamentalists and extremists have voiced their opinion that this is in some way God's judgement because of an apparent increase in worldwide corruption. Their demonstrations have often led to violent clashes and destruction of property.

'Right now we can go over to John in Washington. John, what is the mood in Washington over the phenomenon of animal attacks on humans?'

'Well, as you can see, there is a relatively large gathering of religious people making their voice heard amidst the distress over the frequent deaths being reported after wild animals have strayed from outlying areas into urban areas and even the city centre. So far in Washington, twenty deaths have been reported to have been due to pet dogs this week alone. The invasion of wildlife raises the number of deaths to triple figures. Governments throughout the world have funded this research program which has advocated setting up quarantine facilities and zones for both people and animals ...'

"Are you sure you want to watch this George?" asked Lucy in Flower Gardens, York's high security centre for the mentally ill.

She was beginning to feel uncomfortable with his behaviour, after all he had hacked his wife to death.

"Flowers absolved are always fluorescent, isn't that right Alice?" said George, spreading the fingers of his left hand into a fan shape.

"Probably George, but we're going to turn the TV off."

"Too many people tell the truth and so will never tell it to the ferry man, isn't that right Maggie...Maggie! MAGGIE!"

"George! Have you had your medication?"

"However you never will maybe will possibly never will be switch on."

"Calm down George. Let's turn the TV …."

"No never, no never, not ever..." sang George. He got up and danced towards the TV and gave it a hug.

'...That was a Public Information Broadcast for the whole of the British Isles. Booklets have been produced by the RSPCA and are also available in Gaelic, French, German, Chinese, Urdu and other languages. Please call the following number if you would like a copy or if you witness any unusual behaviour ...'

Flower Gardens was full of murderers and people who had viciously assaulted members of the public as there was no room in the prisons and no one knew how to stop the phenomena. Where it was witnessed that there had clearly been fault on both sides, the ones who ended up dead died in vain as, in such cases, the police turned a blind eye. That was unless relatives of the victims made it unbearable for the authorities until they agreed to process the cases under duress. The rich in particular were becoming almost completely immune to prosecution. As a consequence, cold blooded murder continued to increase. This had a knock-on effect upon relationships and social justice. People gave up trusting one another, unless they had already created a very strong understanding amongst a tight-knit group of people. Even then there was no guarantee your best friend wouldn't turn.

Even charitable institutions and churches became reluctant to help anyone with any consistency. It was as though love was so strained and betrayed that it had almost completely deserted humanity. No one felt truly safe anymore, and no one knew who to trust.

*

Wang Bin experienced some strange things in the UK, but he did not expect Tower Bridge to be cordoned off as part of an investigation into a mass suicide. Through fear of the increasing worldwide calamities, hundreds of devotees had followed a guru-style leader claiming to be a reincarnation of Buddha, Mohammed and Jesus Christ, a common assertion made by innumerable false prophets and teachers all over the globe.

"Alright mate! Bit distressin' innit!" said a Londoner to Wang Bin when he saw him looking lost.

"Er...pardon," he replied.

"Aw, you're not from round 'ere then mate! On 'olliday?"

"I've come to England to travel the UK and attend my foreign friend's wedding."

"Aw."

"Why can't we get onto the bridge?" Wang Bin asked.

"There's been a mass suicide, slit their own throats, religious nutters!"

"Nutters?"

"They're all wackos, the lot of 'em."

"What happened?" asked Wang Bin confused.

"What 'appened? A bloke called Justin whatsa feller told 'em if they all slit their own throats at the same time and jump into the Thames, they'll go back in time and change the future … well it obviously didn't do any good 'cos everythin's just the same as it were before." He went on, looking at the blood spatters on and beneath the bridge, "They did it near the bridge 'cos it's so old, as if it'd make any diff'rence! Look at it, it's a bloodbath."

*

Pill Jennings, one of the cofounders of the cult, shivered and quaked as he led the devotees into ritually clinging onto the fencing in a line, so that when they did the deed with their ceremonial daggers they would naturally fall into the water. He had to somehow count them down to action and his throat felt so tight with fear he could hardly be heard. He considered how horrible it

87

would be for no one to hear his cue to cut, and when he did it first as an example to the others, they wouldn't notice and someone or something would come and call them all to order. What a tragedy to be the only victim of his own deception, but perhaps he deserved nothing less.

As he counted from 50 downwards he clung onto the fence so tightly his hand was numb. His bottom was pointing downwards and he had his back to the water. He occasionally glanced beneath him into the waters willing the countdown to last a lifetime. In the corner of his eye he could see the other devotees ready to die. Personally, he thought it was an unworthy cause to die for, as he didn't actually believe what he had been teaching on behalf of Father Justin. But, he had been proud to be Father's right hand man and the devotees trusted him to shepherd them into truth. He had a responsibility to hold onto the lie. How could he let them down now! But why should people die for a lie? Perhaps it was too late to go back though. He was now at 10 on his countdown to doom...9...'goodbye world'...8...he would look foolish now if he gave in, they would just think he was a coward, and he couldn't allow that as everybody thought he was an important and godly man...6...'perhaps it's better to die for a lie and for people to believe it was a just cause, than to stay alive and convince everyone Father Justin was an imposter'...4...'I can't do it!'...'yes I can! Be brave!'...2...an energy welled up within him...1...he moved his arm the short distance needed for the razor-sharp dagger to do its job...all went dark. 'Plop, plop, plop,' went the bodies. In the battle for his mind, Pill didn't have any seconds left to allow his final lifesaving thought to emerge, which would have been, 'I will never see my wife and children again.'

*

Wang Bin was surprised there were so many problems in a free country. He enjoyed the wedding and had a high regard for Chris and his wife Michelle, but apart from that he was very disillusioned. No one seemed to be pleasant or happy.

Later that day, he was so burdened and lonely that he just had to share these traumatic discoveries with someone, so he contacted Zhang Lili online and told her about the mass suicide. She couldn't believe it either. Why would anybody do that kind of thing?

Lily told her cousin about the South Lake disappearing at the park and how everyone in Xi'an was in shock. There was also talk of water shortages for general consumption effecting Xi'an and the whole of Shaanxi Province, another unexpected development. Meanwhile, she had acquired a job in Human Resources for a company in Xiao Zhai and was enjoying it so far. She also said she was on the lookout for a job for Wang Bin as she had a lot of contacts at her fingertips.

*

Completely relaxed, Burt's body lay back, face looking up to the blue sky with sunlight reflecting from his eyeballs; he floated amongst his companions who were likewise relaxed and in a variety of poses beneath the gleaming yellow disc; they were countless cadavers bobbing up and down on the saline waters of the English Channel, united in calamity, having passed from 'normality' into eternity.

*

Los Angeles was reeling at the damage caused by an earthquake several months before. Wealthy Hollywood residents had been caught in the chaos too. Their implants, plastic surgery and sparkling teeth held no weight when negotiating a deal with disaster; neither could they enhance their chances of survival. The famous fell from their high perches into dust and oblivion.

Six Months Later

Wang Bin and Zhang Lili vowed to support their family during the drought. The drought in Xi'an was worsening and supplies of water from other provinces were also running dry. Fire crackers were heard throughout each day, in a desperate attempt to obtain some kind of resolution. They thought it was worth a try. If they could only chase away the bad luck and show respect for their ancestors by burning money on the street pavements regularly, then someone or something may come to their rescue! Thousands of university students who had never observed these rituals were beginning to do it with sincerity.

Wang Bin, Zhang Lili and their relatives started to live together so they didn't have to face it all alone. They had to be on hand for each other as much as possible. Regular trips to standpipes and aid centres was their only way to survive. Their clothes were all dirty as water had to be conserved for drinking. Many had moved closer to the rivers surrounding Xi'an, but they had all dried up. The mothers and grandmothers who used to crouch beside the running water with items of clothing now simply crouched together in the same locations in circles gossiping and awaiting whatever may befall them.

CHAPTER 12

Car Accident

News Report

'Protests continue throughout the world as a newly established consortium of countries agrees to boost Israel's plan to build a temple in Jerusalem. In spite of this, the various Jewish groups and leaders continue to seek agreement on the ceremonies and laws to be established when the building is complete. Most agree that a system of animal sacrifice on the scale of Old Testament times would be impossible, especially in view of the present world crises and food shortages.

'Many delegates from the western world continue to urge the committee to use the design given in the Book of Ezekiel as a basis for the temple and ceremonial functions. Out of respect for the Christians' association with the Holy Land, building is to start just after Christmas.

Six Months Later

"Look at me! LOOK AT ME! I dare you to look down to the floor – look me in the eye! Do you see just a person, the man next door? No, what you see is a deity. Do you really want to defy me? Do you know where I come from? If you don't, one day you will, and then it will be too late. Come to me now and I will give you salvation. I am invincible, indestructible, impressive and fearless. Will I flinch if you wave a knife in front of my face? No! I dare you to threaten me and my powers."

A man of about thirty years of age jumped up onto the stage with what looked like a knife and intent on killing the speaker. Shep Grifford, the latest self-styled Messiah in Los Angeles raised his chin; he looked at the man and shouted into the microphone, "Come orrn!"

The slightly scruffy looking member of the audience tentatively walked towards the speaker, but before he could reach him, he collapsed into a heap with his bottom stuck up in the air.

"Come on! Where is your venom now? Get up! Get up!"

shouted Grifford.

The crumpled body didn't move. Everyone in the auditorium gasped.

"Do I flinch at threats?"

"NO!" shouted the audience.

"Am I the Messiah?"

"YES!" cried the audience.

"Only yesterday a gang of youths surrounded me and said to me...'Hey, you're that Messiah dude!' I said to them, 'Yep, you're right, you're looking at him, why don't you worship me?' You know what? They found that funny, and one of them got out a gun and was about to shoot me. I said, 'Be careful with that bud, you might hurt yourself, you're dealing with something much bigger than you know.' Guess what!" said Grifford, "They laughed in my face! And I thought, 'You'll be laughing on the other side of your face in ten minutes.' After trying to persuade them and warn them for ten whole minutes - because I'm a merciful guy - they decided to reject God. I said to them, 'Hey you've rejected God, you're going to regret it.' But they didn't listen, they just laughed and laughed. The guy pulled the trigger and as you can see, I'm still here!"

The crowd cheered.

"Just look at me! I'm completely intact!"

The crowd cheered louder.

"Do you know what happened? You guessed it, my words indeed do come true. People who know me know they can depend on my words coming true. Isn't that right?"

The crowd cheered again.

"The man pulled the trigger AND THE GUN BLEW UP IN HIS FACE! Didn't I tell you? Didn't I tell you I'd said to that gang of youths, 'Don't you pull a gun on me or you'll be laughing on the other side of your face!' And what happened? His mouth blew off his face and round the back of his head. How's that for a fulfilled prophecy!"

They cheered more and more, and aggression was welling up within them. Stel and Michael Keeper were beginning to feel not only uncomfortable, but frightened for their lives. They had been invited to this meeting by a trusted friend, so they had hoped it was going to at least be a genuine godly speaker. They obviously couldn't trust anyone's advice any more. Instead, the speaker was in fact a false prophet and even a false Christ. There were so many of these people throughout the Americas, Asia, Europe, Africa and Australasia, and because of the desperate situation in the world, people were looking for something to rely on, especially in Los Angeles after the devastating earthquake that killed 600 000. The Keepers had fortunately been staying with friends outside the worst hit areas at the time of the earthquake, but they had lost many friends in the disaster. The Keepers began to look for an exit. They fumbled through the crowds and occasionally saw people stare at them accusingly as if to say, 'Where are you going? What are you afraid of? Are you an enemy of Shep the Messiah?' This impression made them even more determined to make a quick getaway.

Some others in the congregation were also having serious doubts about this weird yet magnetic personality. But then the people watched in horror as the body of the man who had brandished a knife and crumpled to the floor began to ignite. They saw him move slightly and then heard him scream as he became engulfed in flames.

"Do you know me yet?"

"YES!" shouted the crowd.

"Are you my disciples?"

"YES!"

"I am the Christ, I am the Messiah, I am the Chosen One!"

Grifford had his rich sponsors as did many of the Gurus and Messiahs. Even though people didn't always believe their words they tended to adhere themselves to a particular famous figure. If you could gain a personal audience with one you were almost a star yourself. Associating with a rich religious Messiah also gave you the appearance of godliness and respectability. It also gave you a crutch as many feared wars and international conflicts threatening the very existence of humankind.

Stel and Michael were beginning to panic. They wanted to get out of the gathering and back to their son Trad who was at home. He was their priority in such an evil world. "Why are people falling for this evil. He's nothing like the real Jesus. These people must be mad!"

They eventually noticed an exit in the distance but were worried because the doormen were like trained assassins. How were they ever going to get out?

"Just act normal," suggested Michael to his wife.

"What's normal here?" she replied, convinced nothing they did or said would be acceptable to the body guards.

"I don't know, just say you need the bathroom or something."

"Great suggestion! What if they say it's at the other end of the auditorium? What am I going to say? 'Oh I'm terribly sorry, I was just lying because I think your leader is a lunatic and you look like a wild boar about to gore me because I'm not as sick as you are.' Do you think that will work?" she said.

"You could give it a go."

"Less of the humour, let's get out of here!"

Michael and Stel walked quickly towards the exit. As the exit drew closer, so the slabs of beef on legs became bigger and stronger. Michael uttered a quick prayer for God to get them out safely.

"Where do you think you're going?" said the doormen.

"To the bathroom," replied Michael.

"There isn't one," retorted the men.

"Oh, we'll just have a pee outside then!" shouted Michael not being able to control his anger and fear. He felt dizzy and afraid; his eyes went blurred and he didn't notice the exit was in full view and the men were no longer blocking the doorway. Stel grabbed his arm tight and dragged him outside. They ran.

"How did we get out?" asked Michael.

"Didn't you see? They had to go and tackle a man with a gun."

"That was an answer to prayer, I didn't think we were going to make it," said Michael.

"Watch out! Act normal ... again," said Stel as there were other body guards loitering around outside between the cars in the dark. Michael didn't feel afraid anymore and was quite excited about how God was going to get them out of this one.

They found their car and were so relieved to get in. A couple of body guards looked as though they were walking quickly towards them, but they drove through the complex gate without any problem.

They breathed a sigh of relief, although Michael kept looking back in the rear view mirror to check if there were any cars following them. They were okay; they got back onto the dark country road. Then suddenly, 'BANG!' The car hit something. Michael went dizzy and confused again, "What was that!" he warbled, his whole body shaking. Stel didn't know but suggested he reverse the car. "No, I might run over it, whatever it is." Michael got out barely able to walk and noticed two huge dark eyes staring up at him. On a second glance he could tell it was a stag. He didn't know whether it was dead or not but he wasn't going to stay to find out. Stel watched him as he tried to drag the animal to the side of the road. When he got back into the car his arms felt so weak he couldn't grip the steering wheel, so Stel drove him home.

Christmas, Five Years Later

Chris held his little newborn baby girl. She was a beautiful gift almost small enough to be contained in his two open hands. This earned her the nickname Tiny, which they were going to use until they could agree on a permanent name for the birth certificate. For the time being she was called Tiny Carter. She was also nicknamed Chris' little Christmas Cracker.

Michelle entered the living room with a satisfied smile. 'It can't get much better than this, my dream husband and a gorgeous baby daughter. I always wanted a dream princess,' she thought, 'My little Princess Tiny.' She sidled up to her husband. This simple event was just the beginning of a marvellous future and nothing was going to stop it!

Michelle began to look back over the previous five years or so, and how Chris became a very successful and popular teacher earning him a good permanent position in 'Bold St. Andrew's Primary School' in Winchester, which was ideal for Michelle as she wanted to live in her home town to be near her parents who were struggling to come to terms with the regular worldwide calamities. Her parents were attending Chris' church from time to time and praying for the world, which gave them a focus.

*

One day, Michelle's Mum and Dad were looking after their precious granddaughter while Chris and Michelle went out to do some Christmas shopping. Michelle's parents decided to go shopping themselves and put Tiny in her secure baby seat at the back of the car. She was so small!

Also on the road was Jenny Cartright feeling so smug. She had manipulated her boss into giving her a promotion in place of 'decent Doris' who was the company's favourite lapdog. Jenny didn't mind using her body to get what she wanted and the boss wasn't worried either as he had a secure position within the firm and felt indispensable.

Jenny's husband, Captain Cartright, was the British Royal Navy ship's commander on HMS Bruce. Jenny was unaware of the fact that her husband had just been shelled through the heart while defending his country against King Roald and his forces in the Kingdom Battle. There he lay, splayed out on the deck with a burning hole in his chest.

Laughing to herself behind her driving wheel, Jenny arrogantly blew on her horn at an elderly man who was driving his brand new Effrontero so slowly it reminded her of the story of the Hare and the Tortoise. Like the hare, confident in her own success, she had to give just one more smirking glance at the old codger as she swerved past him just before the traffic lights. But she forgot the ending of the fable.

Mary, Michelle's Mum, reminded her husband he should not go through an amber light, and only keep driving if he had already gone over the line. He was confident he was safe to go for it, but he quickly braked to a standstill in obedience to the rules of the road and his wife's rebuff.

However, Jenny Cartright thought the car in front was continuing through the lights and didn't notice it brake, so her disengaged mind attempted to stop her car up to the line immediately after overtaking the old codger. The ingenious mechanical construction consequently attempted to fill the space occupied by Mary's car ... CRASH!

Mary's car was so jolted that her head bashed the windscreen and started to bleed. There was commotion in the car as Michelle's parents came to terms with the unexpected blast into nether land. In desperation Mary checked on Tiny in the baby seat and breathed a sigh of relief when she noticed the seat was still intact and positioned correctly facing away from her.

But a moment later, at a second glance, she saw some dark liquid under the baby seat. At first she wondered if blood had dripped down from her own face when she checked on her granddaughter, but then she realised she hadn't leant that far back. She thought she had better check the little one properly. She couldn't process what she saw. Michelle's Dad had left a hacksaw on the back shelf of the car.

Chris' church were so unsympathetic over the death of their baby and he was wondering if there were any sincere Christians in the world any more. He tried to confide in the Assistant Pastor.

"We have enough problems, as you know, the Pastor has just been questioned over allegations of assault!" was his response.

"But he might be guilty, whereas the death of my child was a horrid accident!"

"Was it? It sounds more like careless driving to me!"

"What's that supposed to mean? My wife needs help. She can't forgive her parents for what happened, she will never trust God. Please try to have a word with her. You are the Assistant Pastor!"

"Well, when she can forgive her parents, I will visit her ..."

Chris couldn't believe what his church had turned into. 'Where are the Christians? Where is God? Why did he take away my little princess and crush my wife's heart?'

CHAPTER 13

Filiality Day

News Report

'The new temple in Jerusalem is near completion. Many Western and Middle-Eastern politicians see this as a positive step towards reconciliation throughout the Middle East and indeed the whole world ...'

*

In Jamaica, Joe and Edwina took their unusual offspring with them to have Christmas dinner with friends. They had traditional gungo peas and rice accompanied with chicken and curried goat. They all enjoyed Edwina's rum soaked Christmas cake. Afterwards, they returned home, made some strong coffee, and Joe turned on the news.

Joe and Edwina sat snuggled together on the sofa and Edwina put another chocolate in her mouth as the newsreader described the new temple structure which was due to be completed in a few months. Preparations were under way for joyous celebrations on completion of the temple before Christmas next year.

Their strange child was playing in the corner of the room in his pyjamas hoping he was not instructed to go to bed. He had a 'vision' while the TV was on. He saw himself sat in the temple speaking blasphemies against God. He stood inside the temple and declared, "I AM GOD." Around the temple walls crawled all manner of creeping reptiles and amphibians in green slime while his own body appeared radiant.

Joe and Edwina noticed him staring at the living room wall fixated and absent. Last year he had been given a preliminary diagnosis of Autism by their doctor, and this was just further confirmation of the diagnosis. They got up from the sofa and held his arm saying, "Come on Christaff, it's time for bed." They gently tried to steer him towards the living room door but his body was fixed. It was as though his body had rigor mortis and was at the same time glued to the floor. The child's expression didn't change and his eyes remained unblinking. Then all of a sudden, he was freed from the statue-like state and his limbs became pliable again. He didn't look up at his parents but he allowed himself to be led up to bed.

Christmas, One Year Later

The temple opened with a bang during a new holy period called Filiality Day, which would become an annual celebration of rejoicing marking the completion of the Jewish temple millennia after its destruction. Israel called upon the whole world to observe this day as a time of rejoicing.

Heads of State, Mayors, Prime Ministers, Royalty and myriads of Jewish people assembled to witness the consecration of the temple. Prince Jasper fulfilled a similar role to Solomon millennia before by offering praise and prayers of blessing. Hundreds of musicians played electric cymbals, harps and lyres as well as various wind instruments. They were arrayed in fine linen costumes and played in unison. Although most people were unaware, smoke machines had been set in place to symbolise the presence of God. However, they all failed much to the distress of the organisers.

The altar had already undergone seven days of purification and atonement by means of animal sacrifice, so Prince Jasper stood before the altar, spread out his hands in televised view of the congregation and offered a prayer of dedication. Wearing linen clothing, Levitical priests were dedicated as 'sons of Zadok' and offered animal sacrifices. Prince Jasper then recited quotations from the Hebrew of the Book of Ezekiel. On large screens an English version of the extracts from the Bible were also displayed for the English speaking onlookers:

'I will set them in their land and multiply them, I will set my sanctuary in their midst for evermore. My dwelling place shall be with them. I will be their God, and they shall be my people ...'

After the proceedings, the Prince ceremonially entered the temple by the Eastern Gate after which time it was inaccessible to anyone but the Prince.

Never had international support been so strong for the Jewish people since the establishment of the State of Israel in 1948. The sacrificial and ceremonial system had begun.

Although security was on high alert, three local terrorist groups plotted and planned to profane the new temple, and awaited the right time.

Worldwide disasters increased immediately after the official opening of the temple and no one knew why. Another unexplainable event was a plague of frogs invading the temple both inside and out causing disruption during the proceedings.

Two And A Half Years Later

Things began to change. There was a pervasive and oppressive atmosphere throughout the world. At this time, Christaff was moved to Israel with his family due to connections with the country and Edwina and Joe were determined to be the Jews they always should have been. Entry to Israel was stringently monitored, and only those with strong evidence of Jewish ancestry were given clearance.

This was the new beginning the Olivers had been longing for, and Israel was at that time as safe as anywhere else in the world!

*

Christaff thought the false prophet was weak. His child-lip curled as he listened to the imposter attempt to deceive his followers. He thought the deception was too obvious to deserve the attention of any reasonably intelligent mortal. This self-professed Jewish Messiah gathered a plethora of followers. His 'miracles' were more convincing than many others. Israeli police guarded the open-air auditorium and no one was injured while Rabbi Nathaniel claimed to be a modern-day Noah who would deliver God's people from tribulations and the flood of disasters.

*

For three consecutive years Japan had experienced severe tsunamis so bad that the entire eastern side of the country was uninhabitable. China took the brunt of the burden of relief aid and took the majority of the refugee overspill. South Korea took the second largest refugee contingent to support Japan during its crisis.

*

Global use of the French language was becoming almost completely abandoned. Canada adopted English and Mandarin as their two official languages. This was a knee-jerk reaction to what had become nick-named 'Cod-eye disease', which affected the extremities of the sufferer's face such as the eye-lids, lips and ears. It sometimes ate away at the nose and fingertips.

Rumours claimed it started with Christians in France as the first victims were Catholics living in the picturesque village of Fleur. Because of this, Christians were called 'Cod-eyed Christians' as an insult. In every nation of the world there was bitterness towards Christians who were labelled 'troublemakers', unlike the 'respectable' false prophets and Christs who had the support of the rich and famous. As Christians condemned the false teachers, they were counter attacked by false prophets who 'prophetically' blamed them for the worldwide chaos. This became the fashionable view.

Partly as a result of this ostracising of Christians, France became a hub and a haven for people who believed the Bible. There seemed to be less hatred of Christians in France than anywhere else in the world as the Christian community was well respected and the French knew the accusations were unfounded. However, the country was not without its problems, not least the spread of Cod-eye disease. No one knew the origin, cause or cure. Research facilities were overstretched and the rest of the world was reluctant to fund it so long as the disease remained in France.

*

Jinny and Frank had remained in France and Jinny was given support from her local church as she cared for her husband. Telecommunication facilities were down due to years of continual extreme weather, but fuel was still available for transportation. Jinny had driven to Paris for a conference on the Bible, its teachings on the Last Days and how these teachings related to the disastrous events occurring throughout the world.

Most sufferers of Cod-eye disease were contained and supported, but from time to time pockets of victims emerged and the SWAD team, which stood for Swift Action Department, had to be put into action. Jinny was quite nervous as she parked her car on the Parisian street because the city wasn't very busy. She got out of the car but wondered if something was afoot.

Holding hands, the group of Cod-eye sufferers made their way round the corner of Cafe Noir. This style of grouping together was a warning for others to stay clear until they could be collected and taken to the Cod-eye facility. Those with a free hand covered their faces so not to terrify others by their appearance.

Jinny didn't notice they were coming round the corner but when she saw a group of people together holding hands she knew immediately what it meant. As soon as she saw them she screamed involuntarily. The sufferers looked forward at her in surprise and it was the most terrifying sight she had ever seen, ten faces with eyelids eaten away, teeth fully visible due to an absence of lips and barely a nose on their face. She fainted. The group of sufferers didn't know what to do and just stood looking down at her.

Just then, a white Cod-eye recovery van appeared and men and women wearing protective whole body suits emerged, taking the sufferers and Jinny away in the back of the van. One of the suited rescuers noticed Jinny showed no external signs of the disease, so she sat beside her until she came round. When she did come round she screamed in terror again as in the darkness of the van she could see a row of staring eyes. She turned to her side and saw three sets of staring eyes right beside her too. She fainted again for 20 minutes or so, and when she came round she kept her eyes closed and gripped tightly onto the suited doctor, begging her to set her free.

They were taken to a facility on the outskirts of Paris. A recorded voice could be heard in the back of the van for the people who had been picked up. It was in French but Jinny understood most of it. It said they were going to a safe place like a retreat. They would be with fellow sufferers and many had found companionship. They had a rigid timetable to which all must adhere for their own good, but it was emphasised that they would have plenty of rest and recreation time.

Computers and TV screens were in every room but there was no internet connection due to the present crisis. TV signals didn't reach that location either so there was a vast store of films and programmes that were shown on a cycle. They would do their very best to accommodate people's needs and requirements.

Research had been carried out and certain medications had been found to be effective for sufferers. Everyone was expected to take part in the medication program otherwise they may be a risk to others and require isolation. There were over 200 employees, including doctors, researchers and other staff who needed to be safe from infection.

Jinny glanced out of the darkened windows of the van and saw the grounds of a palatial building. There was no sign or facility title as far as she could tell. Actually, she had no idea whether or not this was a genuine government facility.

There were beautiful green lawns with trees and colourful flowers either side of the driveway leading up to the main door. She would wait for an opportunity to speak to someone at the main reception desk and explain her plight. She would pay handsomely for a ride back to her car in the city.

Looking out of the window again she could see people in white clothing gardening. Every so often they turned to look at the van. Her heart sank when she realised they all had those terrifying staring eyes.

She was disappointed when the van didn't stop at the main entrance of the palatial building. It went round the back and stopped at a dirtier and less glamorous yard which looked like the outside of a kitchen belonging to a very unhygienic restaurant.

Two large gates in the courtyard area opened and the back doors of the van opened too. They were all greeted by more heavily suited escorts who led them out of the van and through the courtyard gates.

<u>News Report</u>

'The countless disasters throughout the world have been labelled the 'Great Tribulation'. Statisticians have found that these tribulations are increasing exponentially as though they will reach a climax at some stage. No one knows when that climax will be reached or indeed what the culmination of these events will give rise to. There are many theories. When considering the variety of type of catastrophe it is difficult to attribute all to the same source. While they await the discovery of a single source or common denominator, the theoretical origin is referred to nominally as 'GOD' which stands for 'Gnome of the Origin of the Disasters'. 'Gnome' comes from the Greek for 'the mind' which is used here to indicate a desire to know the purpose behind the mysterious events and their resolution.

'Many equally convincingly assert that it is likely this exponential trend will cease, and everyone will be able to breathe a sigh of relief soon. This is the most desirable outcome as it is estimated that the world's population has decreased by almost a quarter.'

Part 5

GETTING AN EYEFUL

A Watcher's Report

I have been hovering over the world and have gathered an accurate and up to date report of the situation. This is my report:

The situation is ever worsening in the eyes of mortals. After each catastrophic event, whether earthquake, plague or famine, there is no time to take a breath before the next crisis hits the same region. In view of the catastrophes, the thought of the existence of a perfect, all-loving God is blasphemy in their eyes. However, trusting in a philosophy or spiritual belief to see you through is commonly accepted as long as you do not preach a form of 'idealism'. Having a favourite Guru is socially acceptable and is the subject matter of group banter. They compare Messiahs for their looks, quirkiness and miraculous performances. Many false Christs and prophets claim miraculous cures and an ability to predict the future. This gives them credibility in peoples' eyes, so when they criticise the Truth as being archaic and non-intellectual, they are believed.

These false shepherds foretell peace, especially for their own initiates, but in fact the present world will have no external peace. Even internal peace will remain rare. Floods of mortals are abandoning communal worship, through lack of faith in their Creator and lack of trust for one another. Many idle away the days with half-hearted prayers in this corrupt cosmopolitan world.

There are still zealots who are frequently arrested as they pose a 'threat' to what is perceived to be civilised society in which people try to appear positive in public in spite of the negative global climate. Because of the zealots' perceived prejudice they are hated all over the world and regularly executed, and this is seen as a 'necessary evil' for the sake of humankind and their ability to uphold stable positive thinking. To prophesy that a perfect God is allowing these catastrophes to somehow purge the earth of corruption is an insult to modern thinking which believes 'God' wants people to be free to pursue as much 'pleasure' in life as they can. To suggest people are sinners and a cause of the global catastrophes is to their mind an insult to mortal intellect.

The only hope in peoples' minds is for there to be an almost perfect Guru who is politically powerful and respected throughout the world.

Many believers long for God to come and sort out all the mess. Never before have so many of God's people on earth been so aware of what it means to long for the kingdom of God in all its fullness. Never before has it been so hard for mortals to live a holy life; patience is tested to the extreme. More than ever, the chosen ones know how essential it is to invoke the armour of light and to avoid the prevalent orgies and drunkenness, quarrelling and jealousy, which take their victims down an ever-falling spiral of uncontrollable obsessions. People tremble in fear of their own lack of self-control, but instead of finding healing, they feed their appetites wherever and whenever possible.

*

Thank you for your report, it is clearly time for us to instigate the true miracles required to bolster the flagging chosen ones.

CHAPTER 14

Jinny's Isolation

The Harris Hawk hovered over the Parisian landscape ready to descend and seek out some prey for its supper. The bird could feel the wind ruffle its feathers. Its face was confident and resolute. Curiosity hardly emerged in its tiny brain but it heard an unfamiliar sound, a muffled distress signal from an organic source. It was coming from a huge brownish angular man-made structure surrounded by foliage. The bird's priority was the areas of foliage around the dense dark structure where it might find a snack. It was temporarily distracted by the muffled screams coming from the building beside its favourite feeding ground, however, it spread its wings and soared downwards to the left having spied something moving on the ground......

Jinny pulled and kicked. "I'm not ill, I'm not even from Paris! I'd only just got out of my car! Let me GO!" she screamed. "Let me go, I am not ill!" She could not remember screaming like this before, even in the middle of the Glasgow earthquake, when she had been more stunned than anything else. She could not believe this was happening to her, it was like a horror movie. She even resorted to kicking and slapping to break free, but the heavily suited people were too strong for her. She thought of her husband, 'How will he cope without me? How will he cope not having any idea whether I am alive or dead? Even if I get out of here, I can't contact him, there's no phone or internet service. I know, I can go to a police station, they must have some form of communication with other districts in France! But then, if this is a government facility I would be a fugitive, they would send me back in handcuffs! What am I going to do? There's only one thing I can do, escape and somehow catch a bus or hitch a lift back. I will have to make up a story to the driver about being in an accident miles away in my friend's vehicle and needing to get back to my own car. I don't know what else I can do. But it's pointless thinking about that if I can't get out of here. At least I know Frank is being looked after for a couple of days and he doesn't know exactly when I'll be back. So for now at least he is okay.' ....

Harris Hawk swooped down onto its prey, digging its talons into the mouse, which gave a last desperate squeal. Blood seeped from its flesh as the predator's giant beak poked effortlessly into the furry victim........

Jinny bit the hand of the 'spaceman' and she knew she had cut through the suit as she saw blood oozing out. But it made no difference to her predicament. The wounded foe departed and was immediately replaced.

She finally decided to plot her escape rather than fight. That was until she noticed they were taking her into a darkened room. She shouted and wriggled some more but it was impossible to get away. For someone like her, brute force was not going to be effective, she had to use her brain.

They cuffed her to a metal bench where others were also restrained. She worried about the medicine they had mentioned. Were they going to stick a big hypodermic needle into her at which point she would cease to have her own mind?

The suited and muted abominable spacemen looked down at her for a few moments in thought, whatever that thought was, and then left by the same door. Jinny rattled the cuffs a few seconds. Her companions sounded tired but lucid. They told her they were being held for violently resisting taking medication.

She asked why they hadn't tried to escape, but they pointed out that there was nowhere for them to go. No one outside the facility would go anywhere near them and they were over a hundred miles from their relatives with no way to contact them. They also didn't want to pass the disease onto their loved ones. They discussed whether it was a genuine government facility or not and concluded that even if it wasn't, the government may be turning a blind eye because they could learn more about Cod-eye disease if the test subjects were human. They all suspected that the government was silently approving of the centre. Either way, Jinny was going to have to find a way out. Her new friends vowed to help her if she wanted to escape.

"But they need to know where you are and communication may be restored any time!" Jinny pointed out. Her companions said that when they got out of isolation they would write letters while they were still lucid if she could somehow collect them from them and add information about the location, as they didn't know whether they were North, East, South or West of the city. Jinny realised she had no idea either. She had been unconscious for much of the van journey and even after she came round she hadn't thought of tracing where she was being taken. She promised she would get the letters to their families.

*

Jinny had no idea what time it was, but she assumed about twelve hours had passed in the isolation room, during which time she had drifted in and out of sleep. Suddenly the light came on. Jinny only half squinted at her friends although she was becoming slightly accustomed to the horrifying sight of the staring eyes. Her friends likewise only tilted their heads partially in her direction and looked to the ground while they spoke. Jinny noticed that while she was simply cuffed to a seat, her fellow prisoners were dressed in white and strapped into wheelchairs.

"Oh, the disease has affected you very badly then!"

"No," they said, "It's the medication, they have to inject it into our feet and the side effect of the medication is that it rots your feet away. That's another reason why it's pointless thinking of escape, we can't even walk!".......

Pierre was waiting for his bird to return. Then he spied his beauty flying toward him. He held out his arm and they silently communicated with one another, like they had some understanding between them.......

Jinny wondered how she was ever going to escape. Her new friends weren't going to be able to help. If she just made a run for it she wasn't young enough to outrun her pursuers, although they were all dressed like spacemen and that might slow them down a bit. But even then she would need a car with a satnav or a compass at least. So, that was option one if the opportunity arose; she would find the courtyard first, but what about a key to get out of the courtyard gates?

Her companions reassured her and told her something of the

layout of the complex and where to find the keys to the various doors. Options two and three were way beyond her, for example, digging her way out over the next few years, or bribing a guard and killing the rest with a submachine gun.

She pictured herself like a granny-style Lara Croft with her rifle opening fire on the spacemen who were flying backwards with blood splattering everywhere. Then some Cod-eye sufferers loyal to the enemy limped towards her like zombies. Even those in wheelchairs were laughing at her and shooting fire at her from their arm rests; she couldn't kill them with any combat technique! She flipped backwards through the air in slow motion, firing at the Cod-eye zombies, watching them squirm and scatter with their brains bursting out of their skulls all over the place. But the ones with blue arm bands couldn't be killed because of their special medicine making them indestructible.

She hadn't thought before about the possibility of patients being loyal to the facility and preventing fellow sufferers from escaping. Some were probably given privileges in the health resort prison, or should she call it a 'hell resort'? How could she escape the indestructible wheelie weirdos? She found a way in her imaginary computer game. She slung her grappling hook above her onto a high beam, slid up it stealthily and swung to a ledge enabling her to find an opening. But she had to get down into the courtyard without breaking her legs. She jumped onto a series of walls and wooden ledges. She crashed to the floor and was jolted back to sickening reality.

The bolt on the door slid open with a deafening metallic clank. In walked the spacemen. She laid out a feeler, "Err, I don't need any medication. Can you get me back to my car?"

She noticed her escorts twitch a bit when she said 'car'. "Where is your car?"

"Back where you picked me up. I fainted when I saw the Cod-eye sufferers. I don't know them at all. I was just on my way to a conference. You see, I haven't got the disease. Why don't you put a suit on me? I can even help for a while."

Jinny didn't feel as though she was getting through. She felt their grip on her arms get even tighter. It was no use, she knew she was in trouble. As soon as they medicated her that would be it, she would never ever escape, and Frank would never ever know what had happened to her. But she had responsibilities, she had to get back to Frank and her life! She decided to pray in her head and didn't know why she hadn't thought of that before. 'Oh please Lord, if there is any way out of this, please help. I want to be able to help my husband and find out more about what is going on and help those who are suffering. I might even be able to help these people here. It will be impossible to help them if I'm all drugged up and in a wheelchair.'

She was suddenly jerked to the left and round the corner. She saw queues of sufferers, some stood normally, others in wheelchairs. Her escorts increased their pace. She passed a room where some sufferers were getting changed out of their normal clothes and into white suits.

At that moment she still had her car keys in her pocket although they had confiscated her handbag. She knew that as soon as she donned the white uniform it would be the point of no return!

Her escorts held tightly onto her as she stood in the queue with staring eyes all around her. There were only a couple of flimsy screens blocking the view of changing sufferers. She noticed that no one else showed signs of struggle. She however was not infected by the disease as far as she knew so understandably didn't have that same sense of hopelessness just yet.

Behind the flimsy screens she noticed another doorway leading to a room where people were being injected or given oral medication. Entry to one of those rooms would be the end of her. Her legs gave way but she was raised back to her feet by her human 'arm clamps'. Jinny screamed, "GET ME OUT OF HERE!" One of the spacemen slapped her round the face several times. Jinny kept screaming so they punched her in the ribs. She dangled and gagged for air as she slumped down. Her evil escorts held an arm each to prevent her from falling to the ground or running off. When she caught her breath she yelled out again. The escorts punched her in the stomach and warned her they would not stop beating her until she calmed down. Jinny pretended she was sorry and reassured them she knew it was all for her own good hoping they would be thick enough to believe her. This might give them a false sense of security in their success in silencing her and gaining her submission. Fortunately for her they were too full of themselves and their cause to believe she could dare to lie to them.

CHAPTER 15

Fight for Freedom

The spacemen gave her some freedom as she moved behind the screen to undress; she felt like a pig in an abattoir ready to be slaughtered for some perverted appetite. She started to unbutton her top very slowly as her mind rushed to think of a last hope of escape. Through the flimsy screen she noticed her escorts had looked away to speak to a member of staff. She sneaked away from the screen area and crept to a far corner of the room. The Cod-eye sufferers didn't raise the alarm as Jinny was the only one with normal eyes and they couldn't understand why she was in the queue anyway when there was no obvious sign of the disease. Avoiding the glance of the spacemen she managed to slink towards another door. Whatever she did next, she knew it had to be quick because they would soon notice her absence. She went through the door immediately shutting it behind her. Inside the room, there were two spacemen sat at computers with their backs to her. They heard her enter and uttered a few words in French without glancing back. She didn't catch what they said. She thought she had better try and act normal and attempt a reply, "Huh, c'est la vie!" she exclaimed. The two spacemen chuckled. She strode towards some lockers having noticed a couple of empty spacesuits hung up against the wall. Jinny quickly donned one of the spacesuits, including the helmet......

Pierre put the small yet majestic helmet on his prize bird of prey. The bird proudly straightened its neck .....

Jinny then headed for the door, chuckled and said, "Au Revoir," and didn't wait for a response. Out in the corridor she gave a quick glance towards the queues and couldn't see any spacemen, interpreting that to mean they were looking for her. She walked quickly down the corridor and hearing what she thought were running feet, sped into another room. A spaceman walked straight toward her shouting. She was trapped, she didn't know what to do; perhaps it was obvious she was not a bona fide member of staff! She couldn't risk going back out of the room and she couldn't talk her way out of the situation as her clumsy French would be a dead giveaway. On a table beside her she saw an assortment of stainless steel tools. She grabbed one but the spaceman didn't seem at all perturbed. She jabbed the air towards the enemy but the enemy just kept coming. She couldn't read the expression behind the space mask. What else could she do? She jabbed the air again but his hands were almost round her neck. She jabbed again harder and felt some resistance against her hand. The tool had pierced the spaceman's stomach.....

The Hawk shuddered and leapt into the air only for the restraint on its leg to stop it flying away from its master. Pierre gave his prize bird a chunk of raw rabbit meat. He stroked the bird proudly as it sat on his gloved hand.....

Blood seeped onto Jinny's arm as the spaceman silently collapsed onto the floor. Had she killed him or her? She didn't even know whether it was a good or a bad person, but there was no time to waste, she had to escape otherwise it was all for nothing. She quickly secured the seal at the base of her helmet.

The only thing on her mind was survival, both for her own sake and for the sake of her family's peace of mind. She had to get out of this horrible dungeon nightmare and back to her car.

She could see yet another door at the far end of the room. She ignored the quietly groaning white mass below her feet and headed for it. It led to a less clinical looking hallway with walls like old fashioned cobbled streets that were somehow perpendicular to the floor.

She felt like Lara Croft again and jogged steadily through the hallway looking for a way to escape. The ceiling got lower and lower as she progressed forwards and at the same time the small square windows got lower and lower until they reached eye level. It was surprisingly light outside when she had expected it to be dark. Perhaps she had been in isolation longer than she had thought. She could see what looked like farmland stretching for miles. She had to get out there somehow. She took off her space helmet to see better and noticed a fire exit with a breakable band round the handle. She guessed the door would trigger an alarm, but it was the only option available to her.

She quickly replaced her helmet and pushed through the exit door with all her might. Outside, she stood briefly to take in the fresh air. 'What now?' she thought. Jinny could hear an alarm but it was quite distant. Perhaps the system wasn't functioning properly.

The open land in front of her was too vast to run for it unseen. The only lifeline she could perceive was a tractor to her right. She remembered her childhood days when she sat with her Grandpa on his tractor. This one looked quite old so she thought it couldn't be too unfamiliar to drive. She hopped on and brought it to life; it was so noisy! She got it moving but noticed a tug from the back as a broken plough frame gouged into the ground. She didn't have a clue what to do about it so she just bumped slowly and noisily forwards toward some trees on the opposite side of the field.

She occasionally glanced back although it was awkward with her helmet on. She could see white figures in the distance but it was impossible to tell whether they were running or not, or indeed whether they were sufferers or spacemen.

She edged slightly left towards a gap within the dense woodland, but that was a mistake as there were two spacemen stationed there. They just laughed at her and shouted something in French. Again she couldn't understand the accent so she laughed back and turned the tractor round shouting "C'est la vie!" again.

She felt like she wanted to giddy up the tractor as though it was a horse, but her legs were disappointed, so she involuntarily bobbed up and down as the tractor refused to change from a trot to a gallop.

The 'space guards' laughed again as the motorised contraption dragged itself along through the earth beside the edge of the woodland. They saw it stop in the distance and guessed the driver was going to do something about the broken plough. They were disinclined to help as they were not allowed to leave their post and they wanted to carry on with their poker game.

Jinny walked purposefully away from the tractor deep into the woods until she was out of sight, like a spacewoman slowly and steadily trudging through the undergrowth. Once out of the guards' eye shot she removed her helmet and attempted to run with clumsy strides. She saw a clearing ahead but blocking the way was a tall wire mesh fence. She prayed again, "I can't believe it God, you have got me this far and it all has to end here! Why is this happening to me?"

On close examination she could see the fence wasn't very secure even though it was far too tall to climb over. The metal had become rusty and brittle looking. She poked the fence with a stick to see if it was electrified, but then she wasn't sure whether or not wood was an insulator.

She began to wonder whether she was somehow in the wrong about everything. She could have just fled a government facility for all she knew, and she could even be infected with Cod-eye disease. 'I stabbed someone and they were perhaps only trying to help me and thousands of other sufferers! No! I'm right! The facility was either evil or at best misguided.' She reached out her gloved hand to the metal fencing. It crumbled away in her hands. This was the point of her official escape whether she survived the experience or not. Having made a large enough opening, she wriggled through like a frightened woolly sheep.

Euphoria set in and she just ran and ran across the green field without looking back. She was free, she didn't have time to glance around. If anyone was there she would be stopped or shot. Jinny reached the opposite side of the next field and climbed over a wooden fence; scampering through some more trees and out into another clearing, she braced herself for a final sprint into farmland belonging to a set of buildings on her right. As she scuttled forward she saw a solitary figure straight ahead in the middle of the field. 'Friend or foe?' she wondered. She had no choice, she had to chance it. She kept running although she was panting heavily. The figure in front of her didn't move, but at least it was not dressed in white so she wasn't overly anxious about it. Perhaps it was just a scarecrow anyway. But as she got closer she noticed it was a man holding a shotgun with the barrel pointing straight at her.

"Don't shoot! Don't shoot!" she cried out in English, desperate for her request to be heeded. The farmer responded with, "Stop right there or I will shoot!"

She stopped and glanced behind her. There was no one else in sight. Lifting her hands in surrender she shouted, "I'm innocent, I'm not ill, I've been a prisoner held against my will."

As Pierre moved closer to Jinny he could see she showed no symptoms of Cod-eye disease, so he decided to give her the benefit of the doubt. He lowered his gun.

Jinny and Pierre hastily walked together towards his farmhouse.

He reassured her that she would be safe as he had countless hide-holes in his property. He also knew the facility she had escaped from was an illegal facility and had himself made plenty of complaints, all of which fell on deaf ears.

*

Pierre and Jinny sat in one of his central cosy rooms and drank coffee while his house keeper prepared something to eat. He promised to take her back to the city in his Range Rover. He also had a spare can of petrol in case she was low on fuel. Jinny took another trembling sip of her coffee and then broke down in tears. Pierre felt awkward but placed his hand on her shoulder to console her. The Harris Hawk in the corner of the room looked at her sympathetically and shuddered.

After having something to eat and incinerating the spacesuit, Jinny was taken by Pierre to the city centre and her car. "Notice no one is looking for you!" he said. "That shows the dreadful place is illegal and they don't want to draw attention to themselves. At the same time they are not worried about being located and shut down because it is in the government's interests to stay open. They may have wanted to deliberately infect you with or expose you to the disease to study the process of infection from beginning to end."

"I can't believe that place exists! They're treating those people like lab rats. I also can't believe it's still Sunday. It felt like I'd been there for three days, not just one."

Pierre smiled and pulled up by her car. She thanked him profusely and kissed him on the cheek. Even though the conference had not finished she didn't spare a minute. As soon as she had waved goodbye to Pierre, she jumped into her car and sped off.

As she drove, her sense of freedom elated her. She was traumatised by her ordeal but at the same time she felt a self-confidence she had never experienced before. She was however anxious about the person she had stabbed in the stomach. She could be accused of murder! She just hoped that because it was an illegal facility she would not be pursued, although they would have no problem tracing her as they still had her handbag!

Jinny was so relieved to be back home. She entered the house and put her car keys on the hook by the door. On entering the front room, her husband Frank asked, "How was the conference?" Jinny couldn't believe how normal everything was after such a life-threatening experience. Burdening Frank with the details was out of the question in his emotional state. She buried it and simply said, "Okay thanks."

CHAPTER 16

A Time for Everything

December, Six Months Later

It was four years after the death of their little Princess whom they named Jasmine Carter. Stood beside the grave, Chris thought back to the funeral and how hurt he was that his own parents hadn't attended. He remembered himself, Michelle and Michelle's parents stood by the graveside as the tiny coffin was placed into the rectangular hole. When the Vicar uttered the words "dust to dust, ashes to ashes" Michelle's Dad had let out a deep sigh from the bottom of his soul which seemed to echo throughout the cemetery. It seemed to bounce off the surrounding trees and from within the small rectangular hole in the ground beside them like it was a sound box; such was the grief and remorse in his heart. None of them could contain the depth of their loss but the four of them had held hands, a symbol of their support for one another and displaying a sure sign that there was no blame laid at anyone's feet which was a very difficult thing to do. They promised always to remember Jasmine as a part of their family. They also promised to meet there every year and repeat this symbolic act.

Now, four years later, Chris waited for the others to arrive. He couldn't see clearly in front of him as his eyes became uncontrollable waterfalls. He rubbed his eyes and could make out the words written on a neighbouring miniature gravestone:

There is a time for everything under heaven:

a time to be born and a time to die
a time to plant and a time to uproot
a time to kill and a time to heal
a time to break down and a time to build up
a time to weep and a time to laugh
a time to mourn and a time to dance
a time to scatter stones and a time to gather stones together
a time to embrace and a time to refrain from embracing
a time to search and a time to lose

a time to keep and a time to throw away
a time to tear and a time to mend
a time to keep silence and a time to speak
a time to love and a time to hate
a time for war and a time for peace

Chris pondered over each phrase and considered whether the words were true or not:

a time to be born and a time to die

He was in no doubt about the first line. He pictured the day he held his little ball of new life in his open hands and Michelle sitting beside him completely at peace and satisfied with her lot. And then he recalled the screams as Michelle's parents broke the news that their precious God-given gift had died tragically and horrifically in a car accident.

a time to plant

For planting he focused on the digging of the tiny grave before the coffin was laid gently into the ground; he had ceremonially placed a handful of soil onto the coffin lid, wrenching his insides as he felt he was forcing himself to let go of his child. He recalled reading in the Bible that a sown seed dies in the ground before it can grow into a plant and he wondered if he could think of anything positive coming from this tragedy. Perhaps saying goodbye to Jasmine was like planting a seed, and one day Michelle's fear of having another child would hopefully disperse and they could try again.

a time to heal

The birth of another baby would enable complete healing. Although there was no animosity over Jasmine's death, the memory was still causing a lot of grief. Perhaps there would never be a complete healing of the heart. But a new healthy baby would be a help, and Chris wanted his own children with all his heart, and what were the chances of such a tragedy happening again? He decided that he would hold to a New Years Resolution – to support Michelle in having the courage and confidence to try for a baby again.

a time to break down and a time to build up

He thought about his talk with Lily, Wang Bin's cousin, in Qujiang Park long ago, trying to express his concern over the earthquakes round the world and more specifically the Glasgow earthquake and the breaking down of an entire city. The rebuilding of lives and structures was still taking place. How long would it take?

a time to search and a time to lose

Chris remembered the televised scenes of the search in the rubble which stretched for miles upon miles, pulling out bloodstained sufferers with dazed looks on their faces and no strength in their limbs, and the camera's occasional quick glance at the bodies of people who were lost forever.

a time to weep, a time to mourn

He thought of the countless bereaved relatives, thousands upon thousands of fathers, mothers, children, friends; he wondered if they would ever recover from the loss. He thought again of his own plight.

a time to dance, and a time to laugh

Will he and Michelle ever laugh again, never mind dance!

a time to embrace and a time to refrain from embracing

Then he remembered that very strange baby he and Michelle had bumped into in London, the day he had proposed. Michelle was happy for the baby to grip her hand, but noticing Chris' reticence she unhinged the baby's fingers. He couldn't explain it but he just felt he needed to keep a distance from what should be seen as a wonderful new miracle of life. How could he expect God to trust him with his own child if he was so aloof with someone else's?

a time to keep silence and a time to speak

But Chris desperately wanted his own child; it was time for him to face the issue with his wife. He wouldn't leave it for a fifth year and would speak to her soon!

a time to tear and a time to mend

It was time to completely mend their broken hearts, otherwise the grief was going to tear them all apart.

a time to scatter stones and a time to gather stones together; and a time to throw away

Chris noticed stones were scattered upon the grass on the small grave. He slowly and thoughtfully picked them off and held them together in his hands. They were a nuisance and marred the appearance of Jasmine's resting place, so he threw them into the hedge like forgotten memories.

a time to uproot

He pulled out the little weeds that prevented the surface of the grave from looking perfect and filled the little holes with soil.

a time to kill

Chris remembered the circumstances under which Aunt Jinny had recently been incarcerated in France. She had killed someone, but her situation at the time was taken into account, so her sentence had been reduced. She had not wanted to kill anyone and in fact had feared for her life. She had another one and a half years to serve and everyone hoped the present state of affairs worldwide wouldn't give the French government an excuse to overlook her release date. Now communication was much easier again they were going to continue to fight for an early release.

*

Meanwhile, in her prison cell, Jinny looked at her reflection in the toilet pan while holding her nose because of the stink. She could see her eyelids beginning to develop sore eczema-like edges. She must have become infected, either when the Cod-eye sufferers surrounded her on the Parisian street, in the van when she wasn't provided with a protective suit, or later in the institution. She didn't know when but facts were facts, she had it! She was pleased she had ended up in prison now as she didn't ever want Frank to see her looking like this.

She wondered if she should have just stayed in the facility after all instead of killing someone intentionally or otherwise. She no longer looked forward to the day of her release.

*

Eventually, Michelle and her Mum and Dad met up with Chris at the graveside. They all stood and embraced each other beside the grave as was their annual tradition. They prayed as they held each other and gave thanks for Jasmine's short life.

Chris prayed for a new child to come along, not to replace Jasmine but to bring new life out of tragedy.

a time to keep

This was a time for them to strengthen one another. They would keep this memory of solidarity for the rest of their lives, to remember they were to look after one another in such a chaotic and cruel world.

A grey squirrel frolicked nearby. It knew the graveyard very well. Seeing the small group of people huddled together by the little gravestone it wondered if there was a chance of a tasty snack. It waited a while, then it hopped to and fro over the occasional patches of snow until it reached the familiar oak tree where it had faithfully kept its stash of acorns. Scurrying round to the back of the sturdy trunk it paused again and finally settled on a branch.

Michelle laid a small bunch of flowers on top of her daughter's grave and slowly walked away with her husband hand in hand. Her parents followed close behind.

The grey squirrel looked down at the familiar sight from its hiding place, its glowing eyes knowing yet innocent. It was temporarily distracted by a fly which in turn avoided the squirrel. This was all part of the order of things, the squirrel in his world and the Carters in theirs; yet they were linked by location and in a sense dependent upon one another within life's seasons and processes.

Because the group of four people had left the area, a sparrow landed on Jasmine's gravestone and sharpened its beak. Other creatures congregated in the area interacting and communicating. The fly that had fled the squirrel passed by the sparrow which chased the fly and eventually rested on Michelle's car bonnet as she turned the ignition key. Startled by the engine it flitted away catching Michelle's attention. She heard a voice:

'Little by little you will understand, slowly and surely you will learn to walk in the light. Do not be afraid of the dark times. You are worth much much more than many sparrows.'

Michelle's Mum and Dad and her husband Chris were waiting and chatting a few metres away at the car park exit. Michelle hesitated lowering the clutch. She felt very conspicuous, but her family were completely ignorant to the fact that she had heard a mysterious voice yet again. Perhaps she was going insane, perhaps it was just her grief making her hear things because they had just been to the grave. It was almost as though that sparrow had spoken to her.

Pressing the clutch down and engaging first gear she slowly accelerated as she considered how beautiful such a common little bird looked in flight. Its open wings were like the invention of an infallible engineer, so perfect were the wings that the sparrow could effortlessly flit away from danger. And the voice had said that she herself was worth much much more than many sparrows!

Whoever or whatever the voice was it was reassuring and she accepted the message. She would have hope for the future. She had already experienced many dark days as indicated by the first message she heard in Chester Cathedral. Losing her baby was bad enough, so she hoped that this new message was not implying there might be more darkness coming. However, the words did say, 'Do not be afraid'.

She glanced over at Chris again and thought back to the words about resting in his arms. That had certainly come true as had the 'darkness of days'. Even though she took the voice seriously, she again decided not to tell anyone about it.

She pulled up the car beside the others and they got in. Chris noticed Michelle was a bit quiet and asked, "Are you okay?"

"Yes I'm fine, are you?"

"Yes I'm okay, let's go back to ours."

As she sat in the back of the car, Mary thought back to the images of her tiny granddaughter sliced in half and oozing blood. Her heart ached with pain.

*

The Watchers discussed one another's reports. The Watchers were angels who were given responsibility for monitoring, reporting and delegating.

Michelle had to be preserved and her future child must survive the horrors ahead. It was the Watchers' responsibility to ensure that this, and many other instructions, were faithfully carried out.

A watching angel remained with Michelle's car to keep an eye on her and her loved ones. The angel sat in the back between Michelle's Mum and Dad.

The car reached the roundabout and stopped. When all was clear, Michelle took the car out of neutral to move off, but just then a Vauxhall came speeding round the roundabout. It was intended to cause a fatal accident, so the angel made the gear stick in Michelle's car slip back into neutral to prevent her from moving forward, otherwise there would have been a collision.

Michelle looked down at the gear stick, "It's never done that before!" she said, not even noticing the Vauxhall.

"It needs an MOT anyway," said Chris, "We'll mention it if it keeps happening shall we?"

"Did you see that lunatic racing past? He was driving like you!" said Mary joking with her husband and momentarily forgetting the memories that would assault him as a result.

When they arrived at Chris and Michelle's house they had a sombre cup of coffee together after which they discussed whose home they were going to have Christmas dinner at.

Part 6

SEASONS

WATCHERS

A Time For War

The world is at war with common sense and plain decency. Everyone is greedy for more; individuals, political parties, kings, queens, governments, nations and continents are never satisfied. Countries need each other but they don't trust one another; everyone is afraid. Peace is gone, there is no hope. Civil unrest is now a bigger problem than warring nations. Weapons are readily obtainable as law and order has become old-fashioned.

For the next two years every continent will be reeling under the burden of civil war, with people rising as leaders of kingdoms challenging the traditional and ordained boundaries of the world's nations.

Going round in circles, people hope humanity can solve the 'GOD' puzzle, and if not, at least find a solution to the global unrest. Why do they think they can ever solve their own problems? Why don't they look to the True Deliverer? How will they ever be at peace?

CHAPTER 17

New Birth

Over their meal of turkey, sage and onion stuffing, pigs in blankets, peas, carrots, roasts, mash and obligatory sprouts, they spoke of concerns for the future of mankind. They tried to change the subject onto something more encouraging several times, but failed miserably.

"It's the season for happiness, fun and laughter. We need to be positive about the future," said Chris.

Michelle's Mum pulled a cracker with Chris who won the red paper hat, the useless plastic thimble and corny joke, "Make a wish!" suggested Mary. Chris just secretly prayed for a child instead. Michelle won against her Dad and wished in her heart for the chance to hold her own little baby in her hands once again. Her Mum and Dad were wishing for the same thing in their hearts too, but they were too afraid to broach the subject again with their daughter after she went berserk the last time they mentioned trying for another baby.

Cause And Effect

Two years of civil war took its toll, and people established loyalty groups. They submitted to the leaders and regional kingdoms that supplied them with food, as food was only allocated to the highest bidders. There were many worldwide victims of malnutrition, and survival of the fittest was the name of the game.

However, after the two years of civil war and famine, most groupings and regions began to fall back onto a reliance upon the original governments to sort out all the problems again. Governments struggled to do this, but their citizens depended upon them and left them without a choice. Even so, very few inhabitants of the world were grateful and there was no respect for those in authority. By this time, weapons of various descriptions had become scattered throughout every region on earth, easy for anyone to obtain if they desired to pick them up once more for any purpose they had in mind.

Zhang Lili, Wang Bin and their families still struggled to retain a healthy diet. Rice was scarce, but noodles could be found. However, many vendors supplemented flour with other substances from multiple sources guaranteeing an early grave for many. Fruit and vegetables were very expensive and meat was barely obtainable. Countless women, young and old, resorted to selling their bodies for food just to be able to survive. Sickness was on the increase and most of the residents of Shaanxi Province were covered in dreadful skin ulcers.

In Xi'an, Lily and Wang Bin were relatively healthy as they had friends throughout the city stashing food and offering protection, but their sources of supply would dry up soon. Alongside their ability to provide for their family was the guilt of knowing that their well-being meant others were dying of starvation, from young children to the elderly, but every day they hoped for the day when the situation would change and they could make up for it by serving their country in better times.

Disease was prevalent in the city as dead bodies were frequently left unburied. In the early days of the drought and famine, families would bury their own kith and kin, but so many had been left alone and eventually died homeless and friendless.

Several hundred high officials in the city still had access to food and fuel. They kept circulating round different residences so no one could identify them and take them to task. Countless good citizens had died in China as a consequence of corruption holding sway, but no one had the strength to object.

But rain could not abandon them for ever. It eventually came, and when it did come, it came in abundance, from Beijing to Hainan. With hands spread out towards the sky, they used every ounce of energy left in their bodies to leap up and shout for joy. Rolling in the sodden dirt in relief, they cried as their chances of survival had increased in a moment.

It would take time, but life would begin to improve again in China, for a while.

*

Jinny was released late from the French prison. It hadn't been helped by the fact that she had refused to turn up to appeals organised by her family. A couple of months prior to her release she had begun to realise that either her Cod-eye disease was leaving her body or she never had it in the first place and it had just been the unsanitary conditions that had given her sore facial features. Either way, she began to rejoice in her release.

Her husband Frank and their friends arranged a welcome home party with food she hadn't touched for years. When she entered the decorated room in her home she felt a mixture of emotions. Without a doubt she was overjoyed, but she felt strange, as though she didn't belong. Her house had been decorated differently by well-wishers and she somehow felt dirty and unworthy to be free and able to live in such clean conditions. She felt tougher in some ways and ready to face anything that came her way, yet her limbs felt like jelly at that moment and she had to muster all her strength to ignore the grief and pain in her mind and body.

A Time To Love

In the US, Michael and Stel Keeper had managed to keep a strong family unit through the times of global turbulence.

Trad was ten years old now and always up to mischief. He sat on his bed playing lead guitar on his blue Gibson, wearing baggy blue jeans and a black hoodie. He had sky blue eyes in his pale face. He was always content, and hardly ever became distracted by world problems. The only time he worried was when his Dad was doing his space training because sometimes he wouldn't see him for months on end.

Trad's Dad was an astronaut who had been due to man the Mars base, but due to the worldwide calamities and ensuing delays, his position had been given to younger astronauts. He would however make frequent maintenance visits to the space station which was still managing to orbit the Earth.

His Mom used to work in a research lab. Now she was a house wife and presently giving birth to Henrietta who would bring delight and hope to them all.

Trad was waiting for his Mom and Dad to phone with the news, and while he played his guitar, he was thinking of a suitable welcome home poster to put up in the entrance of the house for when his new sister arrived.

*

Six months after the birth of Henrietta Keeper in the US, the Carters in the UK were due to celebrate their own new beginnings at last. They were in the middle of an earthquake while twenty floors up in an apartment block, their new home.

Michelle faced the living room wall and leant against it, bending forwards with her bump towards the floor. She attempted to take slow deep breaths, "Where is that ambulance!"

"It'll come, it'll come....just overstretched at the moment."

"Overstretched! Overstretched! I'll give you overstretched! My belly's so overstretched it's going to explode! Keep phoning!"

"I'll phone again, don't panic," said Chris looking to see where the phone was. It was at the other side of the kitchen. The building had tilted to the side, so he would have to climb up the slippery floor while everything was still shaking.

Michelle continued to breathe steadily as though she didn't notice everything around her vibrating. An ornamental cross fell from the mantlepiece, pictures misaligned and walls cracked. She groaned and groaned like a musical crescendo, with Chris in unison. He was in the kitchen trying to balance and grab the phone. His legs were all over the place.

Eventually the building began to tilt in the other direction enabling Chris to ski to the other side of the kitchen. He held out his left hand towards the work surface to try and grab the phone.

Meanwhile Michelle clung onto an empty shelf half way up the wall, the ornaments having committed suicide moments earlier.

Chris slid away to the right, unable to reach the phone which likewise slid to the edge of the work surface. Then a jolt sent Chris tumbling to the floor. The phone virtually fell into his hand.

The shaking began to subside and he managed to phone again only to be put on hold.

*

Michelle was in the ambulance wriggling in agony. Chris held her hand, his face white as a sheet. The ambulance bounded

138

through the rubble, bumping into bricks and boulders, and reaching a chaotic hospital.

*

On the dusty bed, the mother-to-be awaited the availability of a delivery room. The hospital building shook and her bed wobbled; fresh dust sprinkled her body and gave Chris white hair. Contractions hit again during the wobbly snowfall; Michelle groaned in pain as she endured the agony. "Hang on in there, they said there'd be a room soon," said Chris trying to sound confident.

"I'm going to have it here!"

"No you're not."

She groaned some more and sobbed some more.

Eventually, medical staff approached and rushed Michelle into a room, the building still shuddering. Chris hobbled in after them.

While in the room the noise and rumbling seemed to subside. They felt a sense of calm.

*

When their new baby girl was born, Chris nearly fainted with exhaustion, and something bothered him. He was expecting the umbilical cord to be cut. Not being able to contain his frustration, he eventually spoke out, "Er, shouldn't the cord be cut or something?"

The midwife replied by saying, "We don't have anything sterile to cut it with at the moment I'm afraid."

She saw the shock on his face and added, "Don't worry, the placenta will come out soon and we will be able to cut the cord later. We are just overstretched at the moment."

"She's tiny," said Michelle. Chris didn't know whether she was simply referring to his baby daughter's size or whether she was a bit delirious and was suggesting they had received their Princess Jasmine back from the dead. Then she added, "Tiny little fingers and tiny little toes, like Jasmine's."

Chris wanted to make sure she was compos mentis and added, "We haven't decided on a name yet have we, have you any ideas?"

"No, I can't decide, how about Tiny?"

139

"That's what we nicknamed Jasmine before, how about a different name?"

The midwife blurted in, "What about Tina?"

"That's a good idea," responded Chris.

Michelle agreed.

*

Michelle slept on the ward for a few hours. After a snack and a drink of hospital tea, they had another chat and huddled round their precious new addition to their family. Chris and Michelle were both anxious in their hearts. Neither of them wanted Tina to suffer tragedy like their first child. Chris stuck his neck out by suggesting to his wife that they should pray for their baby right there and then, and if Michelle didn't feel happy about joining in, she should be happy for him to do it. She agreed, even though she didn't believe in God. She thought it was worth a try and that if all it did was give Chris peace of mind then fair enough. Chris gently rested his hand on Tina, closed his eyes and prayed, "Lord Jesus, what terrible days we are in! Please protect this little baby, tiny Tina, that you have given to us. Help her to grow into a mature, beautiful young lady who will be a blessing to many people. Help us to be good and responsible parents. Thank you Lord. Amen."

Even though she didn't believe what he believed and it drove her mad at times, one thing she knew, her husband cared deeply about her and their child. And she loved him deeply too. What more could she want? "I love you," she said to her husband.

Chris sat with his wife on the bed. Tina nestled into the blanket, secure on her mother's lap. At that moment, the chaos around them was just like another world that couldn't touch them.

*

"Hi Mum, here's your little granddaughter," said Chris surprised to see his parents visiting the crumbling hospital.

"Can I have a hold?" Chris' Mum asked Michelle.

"Of course," she replied willingly although she didn't really want to hand Tina over.

"What's her name?"

"Tina."

140

"Oh, why did you choose that name?" said Chris' Mum.

"Because we like it!" replied her son thinking his Mum had a bit of a critical tone in her voice.

Chris' Dad blurted out, "There's no one in our family by that name!" as though it was important.

'How is that even relevant?' Chris was thinking. He felt very uncomfortable having his moody parents present on such a precious occasion. His Mum kissed Tina on the forehead with, "You've got a funny name haven't you?"

Raging inside, Michelle just managed to control her tone of voice with great difficulty and said, "Actually there is someone in our family with the name Tina. I've got a cousin in Australia called by that name."

Chris' Mum rolled her eyes with, "Oh, Australia. That's a long way from here isn't it my little darling?" she said looking at the baby in her arms.

When it was finally time for Chris' parents to leave, his Mum said, "I think you should leave here and come back to our house for a couple of nights."

"Er, no it's okay thanks, we want to get back to our own house." Actually, they were hoping to go to Michelle's parents' house but couldn't say that.

"Is your house safe?"

"Yes its fine, thanks."

"Is the lift safe to use?"

"Yes its all fine, thank you for the offer though. Thanks for coming."

Chris' Dad added, "The sooner you get out of here the better. People are fighting in the corridors, having seizures ..."

"We know, it makes you wonder what kind of world we have brought our child into doesn't it!" responded Chris.

When they left, Michelle just sobbed into Chris' arms. "I'm sorry Chris, but I just don't like your parents."

"I know what you mean. But we have no reason to be upset, they have never really been there for us. We can decide how much we want to see them, and we can't allow them to make us miserable. This is the best thing that's ever happened to us."

"Hey!"

"Apart from marrying you that is."

"I should think so!" said Michelle with a smile.

"I feel like dancing."

"If you do I'll shoot you."

"Go ahead, what're you going to use, your catheter?"

"Hey!"

Chris danced with the bed curtain and pulled it off the rail by accident. They both laughed hysterically.

Just then a nurse walked in looking annoyed and suggested they could leave the hospital to free the bed for other patients. Another nurse walked slowly past the window of their ward and looked at the happy family with a beaming smile on her face as though she approved of their joyful moment, but behind her smile lay a tome of intention. She was Lucy Granger, a member of a secret organisation that had representatives throughout the world. Their intention was to start a new world order ruled by an evil Prince. She, with many others, had met regularly in Jamaica and been instrumental in trying to foster the development of a Prince child, having chosen a Jewish family and impregnated a baby called Christaff with evil spirits. For a while she had to continue to imbue the family's home with controlling spirits. She had also covertly joined Christaff on his flight to London many years ago, having sat on the same plane watching the child intensely throughout the flight from a seat at the back. She was never far from the Oliver family during the whole time they were in London. From a distance she had seen Chris stand aloof from the baby and her spirit guides had spoken to her regarding Michelle's future child. Her child would likely be a threat to their organisation's intentions so she was told she may have the responsibility of dealing with it in the future.

After this, Lucy's mission for a while had been to stay in England and live and work in a mental hospital in York to conduct experiments on those who had been overpowered by evil spirits. This would help with the development of a demon possessed army of mortals powerful enough to defeat the future King of all kings. Her organisation had representatives in all major countries to prepare for the Battle of battles. She had to learn how to conquer and kill mortals that the Creator had ordained for survival. She felt she was gaining some success.

After her stint in York she had moved to Winchester to adhere herself to the Carter family. She had already controlled Jenny Cartright's life to a large extent causing the accident that killed the Carters' first child. She hoped to do the same again.

Nurse Lucy came into the ward laughing and outwardly rejoicing with the Carters. They responded to her politely but Chris felt like he was going to retch. There was that strange feeling again, just like the one he had in London many years before when he saw baby Christaff. Looking into Chris' eyes, Lucy could see he was able to discern her allegiance and knew she would not be able to infiltrate this family easily. She would await future instructions.

*

Michelle, Chris, and Tina's maternal grandparents stayed close and vowed to protect the new child together at all costs. They felt the baby was a precious gift to the world and was definitely worthy of double honour. Although it somehow didn't feel quite right, they often resorted to calling Tina by the name Tiny, Jasmine's nickname. However much they kept stopping themselves it was inevitable after a while, having chosen a name like Tina, and baby Tina was also very small. Using the same nickname eventually somehow felt like they were including Jasmine and Tina in their family together, so they stopped fighting it.

Tina was born at a time when tribulations would begin to subside.

CHAPTER 18

A Time For Peace

Into a world with some hope restored
Into a place with one accord
Going forth with a new sense of peace
For past pain and guilt release

Now is a time for lessons to be learned
Life's values restored and earned
Take hold, don't forfeit the chance
Allow true joy and peace enhance

In Israel, Joanna relaxed; she enjoyed working on tapestries. The Bayeux Tapestry, depicting the Battle of Hastings and the events leading up to the conquest of England by the French, fascinated her, and she wanted to depict her people's own story in the same way. Unlike the Bayeux Tapestry which was actually embroidered cloth, she used traditional methods for her work. Weaving by hand on a loom, she was making her own depiction of a heavenly future for Israel. In view of the turmoil her country had gone through, she felt like Helen from the third book in Homer's Iliad. Beautiful Helen had worked on purple, depicting the battles between the Greeks and the Trojans thousands of years ago. Joanna's work became knotted up, but this spurred her on as she thought how amazing it was that although her tapestry could look chaotic at times, this was necessary for the final product to be a beautiful, colourful and meaningful creation.

In walked her brother Sam with his irritating friend Mark, who would often join her brother in teasing her. Joanna's housemaid Lydia took this as her cue to bring in a jug of fruit juice with glasses on a tray.

Mark couldn't keep his eyes off Joanna who smirked to herself, knowing he was captivated by her beauty. She diverted his attention, "Here, you have a go!"

"I can't sew."

"I'm not sewing, what do you think this is, a torn shirt?"

"Alright, I can't do tapestries."

Joanna went all deep on him, "Whether you know it or not, you're part of the tapestry of life."

"Oh no, let's get away from your strange sister," said Mark teasing her.

This annoyed Joanna a bit but she supposed she had to take the rough with the smooth. She was secretly keen on Mark although she had no idea why. Mark felt Joanna was out of his league and was resigned to keeping a distance. After all she could be irritating.

When they left the house, Joanna crept towards the window to watch Mark leave. Mark was pretending to chat normally to Sam, hoping he wouldn't notice him quickly glance back at the house in case he could catch another glimpse of Joanna. Joanna saw him look and jerked her head aside quickly. She noticed her father's Torah on the sideboard. It was open at God's promise to Abraham just after he had tested his faith and obedience in regard to sacrificing his own son. The angel of the LORD told him not to sacrifice his son after all and promised Abraham that his descendants would be as numerous as the stars of the sky and the sand on the seashore. She loved the story and believed it. She was proud to be one of Abraham's many descendants and wanted not only to bless her own people but somehow the people of the whole world.

*

Chaos in the Christian churches decreased somewhat as people began to stabilise. Many who had abandoned attending corporate worship returned to their weekly routine. It was a time to assess what good could come out of the global tragedies and whether there was something they could all learn from them.

Many Christian Pastors and Elders had fallen from grace, but from within the various churches, new and better leaders emerged, purged by the fiery trials and toughened by the tribulations. One such new leader addressed his congregation sternly.

Mini-Sermon

'How is your soul? Where is your heart? Where your treasure is,

there is your heart. Ego is very powerful, self-preservation has become a form of extreme self-seeking mentality. Do you see the poverty that's around you? Or do you only see as far as your own front door? We have become monsters of our own making, belittling others when our own hearts have become corrupt. We point the finger at others to make ourselves feel better about ourselves. Point at yourself! It is not a time for pointing your finger at the theft, faithlessness and blasphemy of others to ease our consciences. Point the finger at yourself! Do it now! Take your hand and make your own index finger stab you in your own heart and say to yourself, 'YOU are selfish, bitter, unforgiving, unholy and unworthy.'

How does it feel? It doesn't feel very comfortable, does it? Change your ways and repent! Forgive others as you yourself hope to be forgiven; then you will have heart-peace. Say this prayer after me.'

The listeners bowed their heads.

Prayer

'Lord Jesus ... Creator of all things ... please forgive my cruel heart ... I am so sorry for thinking, doing and saying cruel things ... when my heart is dark with pride ... Lift me out of this miry pit ... I promise to change ... I will not turn a blind eye to evil ... I will do all I can to help the sick and starving ... Amen.'

There was silence except for some people sobbing in shame and with repentant hearts. The majority of the congregation of 2000 decided they would commit their lives to living rightly. Hundreds of them were imbued with power from above, giving them all that they needed to fulfil their promise.

The speaker added:

'Put on the armour of God. His armour is not the armour of the world. We are not fighting against flesh and blood, but against cosmic powers which are governing this present darkness, against the spiritual forces of evil in the heavenly realms.

It is the sword of the spirit we use, not a physical weapon. It is the shield of faith, not a physical barrier. It is the belt of truth, not hypocrisy, lies and deception. Stand up and stand firm!'

The people called out, "AMEN!"

Some people were thinking in their hearts that they were comfortable and safe and had no need to make promises, especially since the worldwide disasters had died down somewhat. They assumed a prevalent theory was correct, that the incredible quantity of disasters was just a strange statistical blip. They believed things would eventually go back to normal. In his spirit the speaker discerned what they were thinking and called out:

'Today cannot see tomorrow! Today's light cannot see tomorrow! Today you see daylight, and that light gives you hope for tomorrow. But the light you see now may not exist tomorrow, the things you see now may not be present tomorrow. Don't rely on the tangible things of today for your future. No mortal knows the future and nobody knows when the time of the end will come. Set your heart on things above, then you will be ready for anything and everything that is coming.'

Before the congregation dispersed, they sang a song together.

The Song

I waited oh so patiently
And the Lord inclined his ear to me
He drew me out of the miry clay
And set my feet upon a rock

He's put a new song in my mouth
A song of praise to my God
Blessed is the one who trusts in the Lord
And does not trust in lies

Do not withhold your loving mercy
And let your truth preserve me

148

Let all who seek your face be glad and say
'The Lord be magnified!'

Burnt offerings you do not require
But to do your will
Blessed is the one who trusts in the Lord
And does not trust in lies

He's put a new song in my mouth
A song of praise to my God
Blessed is the one who trusts in the Lord
And does not trust in lies
Blessed is the one who trusts in the Lord
And does not trust in lies

*

Israel rejoiced in its slight relief from worldwide calamities, although sporadic fighting between Israel and its neighbours continued. They felt they had some stability now they had their temple with a significant degree of international approval. After the frustrations of international calamities it was now time for them to firmly establish and regulate the new temple-based laws and ceremonies. One thing the Jewish authorities had decided upon was to determine every Jew's tribal ancestry or identity.

Even though most could not emphatically claim or prove their predominant tribal identity, all were to be allocated one. Having this allocated identity gave specific rights and privileges in regard to education and status, and it became a legal requirement for every Jew wanting to live in Israel. People were permitted an appeal against having a particular tribal identity, but on the whole, the nation was split equally into twelve. The tribe of Dan was not recognised however, due to a disapproval of their ancient history recorded in the Law and the Prophets.

*

Months of relative peace went by in the world and hope was rising in peoples' hearts for some kind of normality. But normality took no account of justice or morality. Greed and self-seeking were still the order of the day, and cruelty was the motive. Relief from sickness, starvation and disease, and safety from animals and war, were the desire of every man and woman. This was developing, but it was not enough to enable them to emerge fully from the darkness, and repentance came only from a small minority. This minority however became stronger and more determined. Whatever may come their way, they were going to endure to the bitter end.

So in spite of and because of the period of relative peace, most people became complacent. Instead of showing responsibility towards one another and humankind as a whole, they partied and abandoned each other, letting go of basic morality and kindness.

As a consequence of lessons unlearned, the climate darkened once again and this embittered humankind all the more; blame was imparted and hatred abounded. Evil held sway again, and the animal kingdom could not endure things any longer either.

*

A Norfolk church reinstated an outing to Lowestoft in Suffolk as it was some years after the devastation from the hurricane and Cholera outbreak. Gulls flew above the heads of the twenty or so children who were playing at the seaside. They played beach ball, mischievously kicked sand and made sandcastles, the structures of yesteryear. They, their parents and grandparents were unaware of what was brooding above them.

Dinah ran towards Robert and Zak who were playing at the edge of the sea. They had been paddling near some pieces of wood. Robert had stood on a sharp piece and was sat holding his foot which was bleeding. Angrily Robert said, "This wood shouldn't be lying around anyway, doesn't anyone clean up the beaches?" Zak tugged at one of the pieces of wood sticking out of the sand. It brought with it a mass of movement from under the surface. What creepily looked like a hip bone emerged. "Ugh!" exclaimed Zak, thinking the wood had some sort of animal bone stuck to it. Perhaps the wood was covered in oil, after all the wood he was holding felt sticky. The wood tore away from the mass below the sandy surface. He fell backwards and the stick fell on top of him, bringing with it a mouthful of sand which he quickly spat out. On his chest lay the stick which turned out not to be wood, but rather the skeletal arm of a human. He ran off screaming away from the sea-edge with the arm clinging onto him, pushing Dinah over on the way.

Between him and his Dad were a group of his friends. They didn't seem to notice Zak's dilemma as at that same moment a seagull darted down and pecked out a chunk of flesh from Jeremy's cheek, and another flew off with a piece from the back of Sara's neck as she ran for cover. Mass panic arose and the children scampered in all directions looking for their relatives as seagulls swarmed around them and sporadically moved in for the kill, picking off as many tasty morsels as they could. As a consequence of the sand being deep and soft, it was like a nightmare slowing down their escape from an evil beast. The children and the sand became pock-marked with blood like a giant uneaten pizza. The next fortnight consisted of calling ambulances, trips to hospital, transfers from one hospital to another and being put on waiting lists. The church decided to cancel any future outings and the parents asked for their money back. Love was cold.

*

The seagull attack signalled a resurgence of peculiar events and terrific tragedies. Humankind went back to their old perverted ways but they became even worse than before with hearts as cold as ice.

CHAPTER 19

A Time To Hate

An angel hovered over the world, viewing the state of the planet. Passing high-rise buildings there were countless homes with shouting voices. Domestic violence had increased tenfold. The Watcher reported this back to his fellow Watchers, and added:

The period of peace was not sufficient to deepen their faith; the rare charitable deeds continue to be a fashion statement rather than a loving act. The chosen ones are going to need a lion's heart.

Nearly 200 chosen ones entered as paying guests into the Roman Colosseum. They then sang songs, prayed and demonstrated against persecution as a message to the world to end wickedness. But thugs were hired by the 'World Harmony Committee' to silence them by surrounding them and stoning them to death – a bloody slaughter televised throughout the world. Would they get the message?

Eighty kilometres south of Baghdad in Iraq, between the Tigris and Euphrates rivers, 300 chosen ones were being burnt alive in a pit and their screams went up to Heaven. This region was beside the ruins of Babylon of old. It was there that humankind had built a tower to reach Heaven thousands of years before, and from there God had scattered the peoples of the earth throughout the world, confounding their attempt.

Generations

Families were in crisis. Children all over the world were not only stroppy, rude, rebellious and serial boundary-breakers, they were now instigators of domestic violence often leading to manslaughter and even murder. They wondered why they should obey parents who had no respect for authority or common decency themselves. Parents in turn did not desire their children to be good citizens for their children's sake or for the sake of society, but only to keep as much control in their own homes as possible. But their children could see this. So instead, they followed their parents' example. In many cases, parents took pride in introducing their children to crime and perversion at an early age. The downward slope to disaster was getting steeper and steeper.

How could families have betrayed each other with such ease? Their sense of guilt and betrayal should have been enough to halt their actions before they went too far. But times had changed.

*

Chris' parents were not only unsupportive and brash, but a festering pair of unfaithful predators. They had been introduced to the British version of the police task forces assigned to the cleansing of the world from so-called Cod-eye Christians. The police task forces were paid to capture the religious people who were adhering to a belief in the revealing of a Messiah from the sky. Chris' parents would be guaranteed food and protection for the rest of their lives if they regularly reported on people. They needed to report a minimum of five 'Cod-eyes' per month.

One month, Chris' parents ran out of suspects, but to keep their contract, they had to find another two 'Cod-eyes'. The only people they could think of were their son and daughter-in-law. They were a little frustrated because they knew Michelle didn't believe in the Creator, but they thought they might get away with it.

The form was filled out and processed.

TARTARUS

In Tartarus of the Abyss there is a stirring amongst fallen angels, accompanied with sore regret that they had allowed themselves to be captured long ago when they polluted the world with evil and magic, charming the daughters of humankind. The Creator had cast them into Tartarus and placed on them eternal chains from which escape was impossible. There they remained for thousands of years in gloomy darkness awaiting their punishment that will be decided at the Judgement of the Great Day. They will not be released, but those demonic beings above them located elsewhere in the Abyss may get the chance to rampage upon the earth and wreak havoc on humankind. Those evil spirits stir and writhe with impatience, revelling in the fact that their perverted desire to cause untold suffering is sealed in prophecy.

Apollyon sits with a guise of patience outside the gate of the Abyss under the sea. His head is covered in reptilian dreadlocks; he spits filth from his mouth and smoke snorts from his cow-like nostrils releasing fumes and bubbles. But brooding evil, and plans of victory over humankind and their Creator, continue to be the unswerving obsession of that powerful fallen angel's thoughts, awaiting the time when he will get the key to open the door to the shaft of the Abyss. That will enable him to set free a horrific demonic army addicted to devastation.

*

There are four angels bound at the great River Euphrates, unable to unleash their strength. They receive reports on the state of humankind and ponder upon the future aftereffects of their might in the days ordained by their Creator. 'When, when, when, can we crush with our fatal blow on this world of turmoil where deserved punishment is due and where untold evil holds sway?'

Part 7

SYMBOLS AND SIGNS

CHAPTER 20

Bedtime Story

Chris and Michelle had no idea that Chris' parents had betrayed them.

Chris' older sister's son Jordan was six years old. He was staying over at his Nanna and Granda's house. It was already nine o'clock and time for bed. Chris and Michelle had gone to visit for the day but were leaving soon. Chris had promised to tell Jordan a story before he went to bed, so he had to keep his promise although it meant a late departure.

"Once upon a time, there was a little wooden boy called Pinocchio."

"I know this story," said Jordan.

"You don't know this version. The Pinocchio story is told all over the world so there are some special differences between each version."

"Okay."

"So, where was I? Oh yes, there was once a little wooden boy called Pinocchio. He always liked to tell the truth."

"No! He always told lies!"

"Shush, that's the version you know, this is a different one."

"Where from?"

"The planet Zing."

"Zing? Where's that?" asked Jordan.

"It's a planet much larger than our planet Earth, five billion light years away. The creatures that live there are called Orangey Tangs. Actually, if you accidentally eat one you think, 'Wow! Just like oranges!'"

"You are making it up," Jordan finally realised.

"No, but don't worry, I won't tell them you think that, because they are very sensitive and will think you don't like them. And if they feel sad they start to turn green and no one will marry them. It's a big problem on the planet Zing."

Jordan gave him a disappointed look.

Chris continued, "Okay, back to the story. Pinocchio liked to tell the truth..."

"Not true!"

Chris coughed authoritatively and continued. "But the problem was, every time he told the truth his nose grew bigger."

Jordan gave him another hard stare. Chris smiled and continued. "His nose grew so big he kept falling forwards because it was so heavy. But it was okay because his nose would then touch the ground and make him bounce back up. His nose was very springy. But unfortunately, on one occasion he was running, and when he got tired his nose made him stumble. He had been running so fast that the end of his nose stabbed into the ground and his feet lifted into the air. He was stuck in that position with his feet swinging in the air for six hours while all the strangers that passed by laughed at him and told him it served him right for telling so many lies. This made Pinocchio very very sad because he knew he never told any lies. Finally a policeman came along and accused him of being a public nuisance. He pulled him out of the ground and sent him on his way with a stern warning.

"The main problem for Pinocchio and his nose though was that he kept poking people in the back of their shoulders wherever he went, and they would jump round and say, 'Who was that!' So Pinocchio had to confess that it was his fault. As a result, he didn't have any friends. At school, other children used to huddle together and point at him sniggering. The rumour went round the whole city that he was a liar and that that was why his nose had grown so big. In the school playground, children often used to shout, 'Pinocchio's a liar! Pinocchio's a liar!' and they would run away from him. No one liked him anymore and no one trusted him.

"No matter how many times Pinocchio said, 'Can I play with you?' they would tease him about his nose and say that their parents didn't want them to play with him because he was a bad person and couldn't be trusted. Sometimes the children would run around the playground holding hands, then sneak up on him and shout, 'Liar! Liar!'

"His teachers usually ignored him when he put his hand up in class to answer questions. On the rare occasions when he was allowed to answer a question, usually when it was a very difficult one, the teachers would still be unkind; if he got it wrong, the teacher would make everyone point at him and shout, 'Liar! Liar!' If he got it right they would accuse him of being a cheat.

"When Pinocchio got home, his Mum used to say, 'How many lies have you told today Pinocchio?' This all hurt Pinocchio deeply because he couldn't remember telling any lies, and he loved telling the truth. He wondered if he had got it all wrong and that he was actually a very bad little wooden boy. He didn't know anybody that believed he was a good boy. So he made a decision, 'I will always tell lies from now on, then people will love me.'

"When he went to school the next day he told lies all day and when he got home his Mum said, "Well done Pinocchio, you must have been a good boy today. Look how small your nose has become!" Pinocchio forced out a smile even though he wasn't smiling inside.

"Whenever he went to school, the children wanted to play with him. In class, teachers would smile at him and allow him to answer lots of questions. Even when he got the answers wrong the teachers were very forgiving and friendly saying, 'Good try!'

"Every so often he would forget to make himself lie and his nose would begin to grow again. He would feel so ashamed that he would pretend he was ill so he could stay off school. His nose very quickly grew shorter again.

"This new lifestyle made Pinocchio very popular and everyone seemed to be happy spending time with him. His Mum and Dad seemed to love him more and more. They became very proud of him and said how good looking and popular he had become. 'Everybody's happy now!' thought Pinocchio. All except Pinocchio! Inside he was crying all the time, even when his face was laughing. He began to get confused between smiling and crying, being happy and being sad. He thought he was the only one who was confused about these things, so he had to hide his sadness from everyone. He was more unhappy than he had ever been."

"Why was he so unhappy?" asked Jordan.

"Lots of reasons really, but mostly because he didn't enjoy telling lies. But it seemed to be the only way he could stop people not liking him."

"That's really sad. I don't like telling lies either."

"Oh no, your nose is getting really small!" exclaimed Chris looking horrified.

"No it's not! You're joking."

Chris laughed.

"What happened next?" asked Jordan.

"In the end, Pinocchio died and went to Heaven to be with the other wooden boys and girls. They were just like him, and guess what?"

"What?"

"They all had very long noses!"

"That's silly."

"And, because they all loved telling the truth, eventually the King of Heaven changed their bodies into perfect ones, so they didn't have to have long noses anymore."

"Were all Pinocchio's school mates made of wood too?"

"No, and that used to make Pinocchio feel even more lonely. He thought his body was bad and every other person's body was better. But when he got his new body in Heaven, it was better than all of his classmates' bodies."

"I'm glad I'm not made of wood," said Chris' nephew, relieved.

"But you are."

"No I'm not, you're silly."

"Well how come you float when you have a bath? Everyone knows that wood floats."

Jordan was getting really sleepy. All the jokes and wrong stories had tired him out. His Mum, Chris' older sister, came upstairs saying, "Is Uncle Chris being silly?"

"Yes, very silly. I think he's from the planet called Zing."

"I know," she said. "Shall we send him back?"

Jordan thought for a while, "No."

*

Chris and Michelle were polite and respectful towards Chris' parents for Tina's sake, so she could get to know her entire family as she grew up. Tina's grandparents, Nanna and Granda, were all smiles with the three of them as though everything was normal, but they were hiding a secret. It was the secret of their betrayal, which was intended to lead to the deaths of their son and daughter-in-law, and to their granddaughter becoming an orphan. And what kind of surrogate parents would she end up with? Knowing all this, Chris' evil parents still smiled as their son left with his wife and child.

162

*

In the car, Chris thought back to his childhood. He couldn't remember anyone telling him a bedtime story like he had just done for his nephew. He did remember his older sister spending time with him though. As Michelle drove, Chris thought back to the days when they lived in the countryside. His older sister used to take him for walks into the nearby fields. Sometimes his younger sister had to tag along, much to his older sister's displeasure.

At least he felt safe with his older sister. He was free to explore things such as fish and other creatures in the beck or climb trees and look for birds' nests. He loved to see colourful eggs in their beautifully woven structures, but he didn't look too long and afterwards waited at a distance to make sure the birds returned to their young and didn't desert their eggs. His sister taught him so much. His parents, on the other hand, were too busy to spend any time with them because they were always out making money …

"Hey …..Look at me!" shouted Chris to his sister whilst swinging from a tree branch.

"Be careful!" she responded. "You're too high up, if you fall you'll break your legs."

"You can catch me," said Chris trusting his sister to look after him.

"Mum and Dad'll kill you if you fall."

"Why should I care. They don't care about me," said Chris swinging around.

"Of course they care about you."

Chris was beginning to get weak hands. "Help, I'm falling!"

"I told you!" shouted Veri running to catch him. When he fell she barely broke his fall. He twisted his ankle badly and writhed around on the floor in agony. "I told you, you idiot … Look, it'll be okay, I'll help you walk."

She helped him to his feet and walked with her arm round her limping brother. Chris found a stick on the way home and used it as a walking stick, although most of the time he just poked around in the grass as they slowly hobbled over the hill.

Suddenly he noticed some small brown oval objects in the grass; they were birds' eggs. On closer inspection he could see within the rough grass that there was a beautifully woven nest containing the six smooth 'pearls'. Amazingly, no person, animal or event had crushed these perfect objects that held new life. He gasped at the beauty of it. His sister told him to be careful and not stay by the nest too long or the nest may be abandoned. Even birds care for their young and provide a carefully crafted abode for them, nurturing them while they are vulnerable, shielding them against the storms of life.

The sun was beginning to set as they walked home over the horizon, a hobbling silhouette.

... Chris was more than happy with his family of three, even though they were living in dangerous times. He was determined not to repeat the mistakes his parents had made with him. He would be faithful to his family and make sure he spent quality time with Tina throughout her life.

CHAPTER 21

Jinxed

Back in Israel, Christaff's parents discussed the mental well-being of their child. For the first time, they began to seriously consider whether Mamosa's friend in Jamaica had had something to do with the way their son had developed:

"I think it had something to do with that spirit doctor, witch doctor or whatever he was!" said Edwina.

"Shaman," said Joe clarifying it.

"Shaman? I've never heard of a Shaman before."

"That's what you call them," said Joe. "I don't know whether it's anything to do with that Shaman or not but I don't think Autism is Christaff's only problem. Just think about all the crazy dreams he describes. He's seriously disturbed, but at the same time, he's not really bothered about the horrible things he thinks about. It's like he gets really excited about evil. I'm just worried he'll turn out to be some kind of Hitler or a serial killer."

Edwina was worried. "What does all that say about us? People are going to think we are evil as well if he ends up like that," she said.

"He's our child and we have a responsibility towards him. What can we do?"

"Get help, the best help we can."

Edwina and Joe had faced a lot over the years with Christaff. His peers were afraid of him, as anyone who made fun of him at school ended up having something terrible happen to them or their family. They said he was jinxed. At the same time they had a lot of respect for his intellectual abilities and his school often awarded him prizes and commendations. This was done reluctantly though; although his academic achievements needed recognition, there were other children more deserving.

His parents didn't know it, but Christaff had heard every word his parents spoke. It was no surprise to him, and he wasn't the slightest bit perturbed as he had higher matters on his mind, about which he confided in no one.

*

In Winchester, England, Michelle put down the letters on the board as they played Scrabble in the dining room waiting for Tina to wake up for her feed, "S.H.A.M.A.N."

"Do you know what that means?" asked Chris.

"Yes, a crazy voodoo type witch doctor person thingy me bob."

"Yes, and guess what! In Chinese, 'sha' means 'kill'. So he's a 'kill man'."

"Oh, very good. But it's not a Chinese word."

"Also, in Chinese, 'man' means 'slow'. So, a Shaman is someone who kills someone slowly. Ha ha!"

"I'll kill you slowly if you don't shut up," responded Michelle, annoyed because she was losing the game again.

*

After washing up the dinner pots, Chris thought about his parents again. He knew they were far from being the perfect parents, but he had no idea they would do something like betray them to the Cod-Eye Cleansing police. The first they knew anything was when the CEC police came knocking on their door with stun guns and batons.

Chris didn't know at first, but his parents were waiting in the street below to claim baby Tina for themselves after their son and daughter-in-law had been arrested.

Michelle looked through the spyhole, "It's the CECs! What're we going to do?"

"Follow our plan. Where's Tiny's harness?"

"Bedroom drawer, quick!"

Chris put the harness on in double-quick time. Michelle placed Tina into it and quickly opened the balcony windows. They climbed out and locked the windows from the outside pocketing the key as a crashing sound signaled the policemen's attempt at breaking the door down. Chris carefully pulled at the cord on the outside of the windows allowing the bar to fall across the windows on the inside as though they had been locked from inside the room.

The front door crashed open and the police unprofessionally stumbled into the apartment. Michelle and Chris stepped onto the ledge out of sight, just in time to avoid the gaze of the policemen. The ledge was not only precarious but painful as they hadn't had

166

time to put shoes on. Michelle was wearing slippers and Chris had bare feet. They were facing the wall twenty storeys up and Chris reached for the metal handles he had previously installed for this purpose. Michelle was already clinging on. Chris nearly fell back due to the imbalance of having Tina on his back. Michelle's right foot slipped as she held out her arm to stop Chris falling. Her slipper fell off her foot and floated down. Her eyes followed it and eventually focused on a familiar car. "Your Mum and Dad's car's down there."

"Are you sure?" responded Chris not daring to look down.

"It looks like it. What if they come up and the police accuse them of being Christians and arrest them instead?"

"How can you look down? I'm shaking. I don't think I can hang on any longer."

"Don't worry, just think of Tiny," said Michelle reassuring him. "I'll keep checking to see if the police go back out of the building, then we can go in."

Just then, the windows rattled as the police tried to open them. The police were satisfied no one was on the balcony as the windows were locked from the inside; they decided to leave.

The wind was blowing hard against the family on the ledge. Chris' hand was cold and numb; he couldn't tell whether he was clasping the handles hard enough so he had to grip with all his might. "Have the police left yet?"

"I can see them leaving ... two policemen. That's strange, they're going up to your Mum and Dad's car. One of them is talking through the car window."

"Come on, let's get back in. We might have to do something to help my parents anyway, although I've no idea how without us getting arrested ourselves," puzzled Chris, pulling the key from his pocket and searching for the card to release the bolt.

*

In the apartment next door to the Carters, Jamie was on the phone to his friend Sheila. Jamie's housemate Ben was trying to watch a comedy duo on TV. He couldn't focus while this bizarre mixture of voices was filling the room. His noisy neighbours were bad enough, crashing and banging. Now on top of that he had to put up with gobbledegook, the result of hearing Jamie's one sided conversation and the TV characters at the same time.

'What's that about?'...
"So that's why you're telling me to use my instinct," said the guy with the red stripy T-shirt on TV.
'Oh yes!'...
"Not many people understand what instinct is," replied the young woman with pig tails.
'That's right'...
"What is it anyway?" she added.
'What do you mean?'...
"It means you're very smelly inside. Ha ha."
'Oh I get it, a hound is a dog and dogs like bones'...
The young woman with the pig tails slapped him round the face.
'I bet it's boring really'...
"You've got a cheek," she said.
'Mine's better than yours!'...
'It's just not my thing'...
'Well, I'm surprised you managed to get a signal'...
"Shut up! This is driving me mad! Can't you phone outside?" shouted Ben at his friend Jamie.
"Soz, I can finish in a minute," said Jamie. He continued:
'So can I when I put my mind to it'...
Ben buried his head in his hands.
'Oh this and that'...
    And so the phone conversation continued.

    Michelle and Chris flopped to the floor like a large sack of potatoes. They couldn't contain their exhausted giggles as they tried to release Tina from the harness. They didn't realise a policeman was still outside the door.
    Police Officer Jones took his time. He had no reason to rush. His mind had compartmentalised his job, and the seizing and delivering of Christians was 'just another day at the office' for him. He was actually thinking about his girlfriend, wondering whether she loved him or not. As he pondered over this issue he carefully

and methodically taped the CEC seal over the Carters' broken door with the words 'Cod-eye cleansing. Do not enter'. He wanted to marry his girlfriend and hoped she felt the same way. As he put the neat finishing touches to the seal, he imagined his future family sat round the kitchen table knowing they would always be together. Being distracted in his mind, the policeman didn't hear the muffled giggles and baby's moans from the Carters' apartment.

The Carters decided to leave the apartment as soon as possible, so they grabbed their emergency travel bags and put their shoes on.

By this time, Ben had exited his apartment in a mood with his fists clenched. He just wanted to smash someone's face in. He saw the CEC policeman nonchalantly walking away from the Carters' door, the location of the crashing sounds earlier. Ben caught his attention with, "You alright mate?"

"Yes are you?" replied Officer Jones heading for one of the lifts. Ben simply wrapped his arm around the policeman's neck, clenched tight and wrenched it as though he was wringing a chicken's neck before preparing it for dinner. Officer Jones fell to the floor, his earthly existence ending.

Ben casually approached the lift to get cigarettes from the lobby. Just then, Michelle and Chris exited their apartment, seeing the policeman on the floor and their neighbour stood in the open lift smiling. They rushed back into their apartment.

*

After a few minutes, the Carters stepped over the body and entered a lift. Exiting on the ground floor, they walked across the lobby as though it was a normal day, passing the cigarette booth where Ben the murderer was chatting up the cashier. His parents' car had gone and there were no police; they must have given up waiting for their daydreaming colleague.

They found their own car in the car park and got in, hoping no one would stop them leaving. With much anxiety and rubber necking they drove through town. They decided that after they had driven a hundred miles or so they would phone their friends who lived just outside Chester, and who had offered to put them up in such circumstances.

*

169

Sheila was lying in the road after becoming the victim of a hit and run. She was semi-conscious. Claire had been flung across the road and was barely moving. Five minutes earlier, Claire had been waiting for her friend to get off the phone, and that one-sided conversation was all that went through her mind again and again as she agonised over whether anybody would attempt to help them. People didn't seem to care about anyone anymore. Again and again like a spinning wheel she replayed the one sided phone conversation she had heard from Sheila just before they were hit by the vehicle:

'I've been watching Sherlock Holmes...
You know, only the most famous detective in the world...
Started with Basil Rathbone...
That's why the Hound of the Baskervilles was after him!...
Basil RathBONE!...
It's good, I'm really enjoying it...
Not if you've got a brain...
So why don't you like old Sherlock then?...
I'm watching it every night...
I can do anything these days...
What are you doing later?...
Shall we meet up?'...
....

Sheila had been stood in the middle of the road, not concentrating properly because she was speaking to Jamie on the phone. Claire had followed her out to grab her by the arm and guide her. A fraction of a second before Sheila had managed to press the button to end the call, a small lorry had come speeding round the corner hitting them both and flinging them apart. The driver had looked at the victims with gleeful surprise; he had laughed and sped off treasuring it as the highlight of his day.

Before he could switch off the phone, Jamie had heard the screams. Shouting, "Sheila! Sheila!" Jamie had then rushed out of his apartment. He saw the policeman strewn across the floor and a CEC seal across the Carters' door, "What's been going on here! Ben! Ben!" He went back into his apartment to get his shoes.

He left his apartment again and got into the lift while the Carters were still in their apartment. Jamie got out of the lift and into the lobby. Not seeing Ben buying cigarettes at the kiosk, he ran out of the apartment building's main doorway to look for his friend Sheila, whom he thought had obviously been in some kind of accident.

As he ran out of the building, Jamie was caught on the lobby security cameras. It looked as if he was fleeing away from something. This visual record would later be used as an easy way to wrongly convict him of murder without a proper trial.

*

Ben wasn't getting very far with the girl at the kiosk, which made him even more frustrated. He stormed out of the apartment block.

Meanwhile, Jamie was still looking for Sheila whom he knew had been nearby when she phoned him. He eventually heard sirens and followed the sound. As he sprinted, his heart pounded and he was unable to breathe steadily. Everyone around him stared in disgust at his display of emotion, as though his concern over someone else's well-being was unusual and offensive. He strained his ears and eyes as he ran and sweat poured from his face.

Round a corner he saw crowds of people and two ambulances. He couldn't see who was injured but feared the worst. Getting closer he saw Sheila's friend Claire being given CPR. Sheila was sat sobbing at the back of one of the ambulances. Jamie went up to her and Sheila hugged him tight. "It's all my fault!" she said. "I wasn't looking where I was going."

"I'm sure it's not your fault, what happened?" asked Jamie.

"We were crossing the road and a lorry came and ran us over. I wasn't looking!"

"Well, what was Claire doing?"

"She can't have been looking either."

"What if she was, and the lorry driver just didn't care. And you were relying on Claire, because you were on the phone."

"It's no excuse, she's dying and it's my fault!"

"Where's the lorry?" asked Jamie.

"It drove off."

"It was obviously the driver's fault then, otherwise he wouldn't have driven off."

Sheila sobbed and sobbed. Jamie noticed they had stopped giving Claire heart massage and someone looked at their watch as if to record the time of her death. Sheila screamed out and ran towards Claire shouting, "NO! NO! DON'T STOP!" She fell over and banged her face on the concrete. The ambulance driver helped her up.

"There's nothing they can do," said Jamie leading her back to the ambulance. The paramedics near Claire's body shrugged their shoulders.

*

From a distance, Ben heard all the commotion. Out of curiosity, he decided to have a look. He peered through the crowds of people and recognised Claire as they placed a sheet over her face. Turning to the side he saw Jamie and Sheila at the back of an ambulance and Sheila had a blanket round her. Ben went over and, stroking Sheila's shoulder, asked what had happened. Jamie didn't trust his friend and stood in objection to him showing affection towards his girlfriend.

But before he could utter a word, two policemen approached Jamie. "Are you Jamie Anderson?"

"Yes," replied Jamie.

"We'd like to take you down to the police station to ask you a few questions about the murder of a police officer."

Jamie knew who they were talking about as he had passed the body outside his apartment. He assumed they just wanted to know if he had seen anything, so he went with them willingly. He didn't know it was going to be the last time he saw his girlfriend Sheila or Ben the real murderer.

*

After an anxious but safe journey, the Carters finally arrived at their sanctuary, their friends' home. They were an older couple who lived in Wervin on the outskirts of Chester city. Chris knew them from church when he was at university.

It was a country house with plenty of lush fields around it. The Carters spent the first couple of hours settling in and telling their friends about their escape. After a good meal and leaving their sleeping baby with their friends, they went for an evening stroll in the nearby fields. They finally felt safe for a moment and breathed a sigh of relief. Chris reflected on his childhood again, playing in the fields with his sister, with whom he felt safe all those years ago.

CHAPTER 22

Soul-Searching

On their third day at Wervin, Chris and Michelle were taking their daily walk in the fields while their friends watched Tina, and the early evening sky was peculiar; it was a strong shade of purple covering the entire sky with no shade variation. It was the first time anyone in the UK had seen a sky quite like that. This phenomenon stretched across the world for 48 hours. It was like a blank canvas onto which a new world would be painted, the greatest masterpiece of all time.

Chris had insisted on taking out one of their friends' loaded shotguns on their walk for protection. Michelle was worried in case Chris was becoming a different person, one who was willing to kill another human being. 'What if he loses control?' she thought. On the other hand she felt a degree of safety, having her courageous husband at her side.

Meanwhile, General Swatter in charge of the southern England CEC police unit had to fill his quota. With the absence of the young Carter family, Chris' parents were two Cod-eyes short of their contracted quota. This meant they had to take their place. Chris' Mum and Dad were gagged and blindfolded in the shooting station. They were in the middle of a line of 40 prisoners. Trembling, they felt unjustly treated, and when Mrs. Carter eventually finished biting through the muzzle, she cried out, "Wait, I'm innocent!!"

One of the shooters muttered, "No one's innocent these days darlin'!"

The command was given and the deed was done. All 40 were shot clean through the heart. The shooters had had a lot of practice and this was 'just another day at the office'.

*

Chris' head touched the pillow and deep sleep overtook him.

Outside, the blank purple backdrop stretched across the sky above him and around the horizon. Everything was still and silent. Nothing moved until he heard wings flapping beside him. A dark bird rose up, a silhouette flying into the purple backdrop. All of a sudden, birds of various colours, shapes and sizes appeared from all directions, flying, flitting and gliding in the sky. Among them were birds representing many countries and cultures, such as a pair of Rainbow Lorikeets from Indonesia and the eastern seaboard of Australia displaying colours of blue, orange, red, green and yellow. There was the shy Painted Bunting from North America, the poor-flying Keel-Billed Toucan from Latin America and the Golden Pheasant from China. The beautiful red, yellow and blue Scarlet Macaw also spread its wings across the purple sky. Amongst their companions were different varieties of Kingfisher and Humming Bird. Red Kites with forked tails and two-metre wingspans looked stunning as they soared across the sky. Clumsy Peacocks displayed every colour imaginable. Birds of Paradise flew from all directions mingling with the varieties of species.

Very soon, hundreds, then thousands of birds had gathered and were moving throughout the space above. They were beautiful and clear, from all over the globe, displaying perfect colourful shapes.

A pure, snowy white dove flew overhead. Then, Chris WAS the dove. He was safe, significant and secure. But where were Michelle and baby Tina? Chris woke up with a start as Michelle lay beside him. "Shell, Shell," whispered Chris nudging her gently. She was fast asleep. It was only three o'clock. He decided to let her sleep, and switching on his bedside lamp, he jotted down on paper what he had just dreamt as he felt it was somehow very significant. As he wrote he felt strongly that this was a message to give to Michelle to reassure her and their child in the future. He felt that if something were to happen to him, Michelle and Tina would not be alone even if they felt alone at times. He couldn't understand why he had to tell Michelle this because he had never had a special dream like this before. Dreams were usually just pictorial impressions of the way he was feeling that day or that week. But he knew he had to tell her as soon as possible that everything was going to be alright. He guessed it could wait until the morning. He looked at his wife sleeping peacefully under the covers beside him and a feeling of awe came upon him. 'I love you so much,' he thought. 'I would give anything to protect you.'

When his mind stopped buzzing, he lay down his head once more, but he couldn't help thinking, 'If I am that dove, where am I going?'

*

Morning came. Tina was still asleep and Michelle was eating cornflakes at the kitchen table. Chris sat down facing her with a glazed expression.

"What's up with you?" asked Michelle with a smile.

"I had a strange dream last night."

"What about? Pink elephants in pyjamas? Getting a well-paid job as a groundsman? Being married to Madonna?"

"Not far off the first one you mentioned."

"Oh, this sounds good," she said sarcastically.

Chris tried to explain it the best he could:

"Well, you know that purple sky we saw yesterday?"

"Yes."

"Well, it was like that, but everything was really quiet, not a single sound, until I heard a bird flying at the side of me. And then, eventually, loads of different varieties of bird started to fill the purple sky. And there was a beautiful white dove flying over my head. Then, I WAS the dove."

"That's because you're a sweety."

"So, as a dove, I realised I was on my own. I was wondering where you and Tina were. Then I woke up and felt I had to tell you you didn't have to worry."

"I am worried, I'm married to a bird."

"I know you think I'm mad, but I just want to say, if one day something happens to me and I'm not there, don't worry, you won't be on your own somehow. You and Tina will be okay. I can't explain it, but I just believe I have to tell you that. Right, what's for breakfast?"

"Bird seed obviously."

Although Michelle gave her husband the impression she wasn't taking his words seriously, she pondered over his words throughout that morning and at the back of her mind worried about what might happen to Chris. Then she realised that worry was the opposite of what the message was trying to produce. So, she was not to worry at a time of some sort of separation, whatever form that took, if it happened.

Something like that must be due to happen otherwise what was the point of God or whatever it was passing on the message? 'Oh it's so confusing!' she thought. She decided that Chris was either being a bit daft or if it was some supernatural message it wasn't necessarily anything major to worry about. After all, it did say we were not to worry. Worrying about what might happen was not helpful at that moment; she was more concerned about keeping their location secret so that her husband didn't get arrested for being a 'Cod-eye'.

Dread filled her heart all of a sudden. Perhaps that's what the message was referring to! Perhaps her husband was going to be found and executed. Then she would be alone! She thought back to the bizarre messages she had received and kept secret from Chris. The first one in the Cathedral had referred to dark days, the second one in the cemetery car park, to dark times. In fulfilment of the first message, she should not forsake her family and she would remain faithful to her husband. According to the second message, she was not to be afraid. So that was it, she would be faithful and strong for her family and look after them as much as possible, and not be afraid of whatever happened, as someone or something would look after them. In the meantime, she would not try to imagine what may or may not happen to Chris. She would hold him tight in her arms.

*

After Claire's death and Jamie's arrest, Ben was the only friend Sheila had at the time. She tried many times to pluck up courage to get information from the police about Jamie, who never returned from the police station. Ben was happy not to push for information in case it somehow made the police consider him as a murder suspect. He pretended to sympathise with Sheila just enough for her not to suspect he didn't care about his friend.

There was a very real danger in those days of becoming a scapegoat or of being falsely accused, but Ben's lack of courage disappointed Sheila; she guessed cowardliness was the simple reason for his inaction. Hopefully, they would release Jamie when they found the real culprit. Ben had no intention of handing himself over to the police. 'It's a case of survival of the fittest,' he thought.

None of their group had any relatives that cared about them. They had become a sort of family together. Now one of them was dead and one was in the hands of the police. They didn't have any money to speak of and had no support in a crisis.

As time went by, Sheila and Ben became very dependent on one another, although Sheila felt uneasy around Ben; she just put it down to him being a particularly selfish person, more so than Jamie, and him not being her ideal man.

One evening, Ben and Sheila were returning from a night club. Sheila was particularly inebriated, but Ben, being able to hold his drink better than Sheila, guided her home through the dark, dangerous streets. He knew she didn't particularly trust him or even like him, and in spite of this and his crimes, including his ability to kill without compunction, he still felt a duty towards Sheila and wanted to protect her.

He wondered if his eyes were deceiving him but he could see the dark sky above him occasionally flash and light up with a variety of colours. He had never seen this before, although he had seen the peculiar purple sky before. This was a new phenomenon to him. He put his arm around Sheila's shoulders to stop her stumbling while he gazed up at the Aurora Borealis, struck at the awesome mysteries of the universe. It made him feel special to be even a small part of the order of things, and at the same time he felt insignificant in comparison to the size and power of the cosmos.

This experience gave rise to a soul-searching in his heart and mind. His sense of awe and wonder didn't somehow sit easily with his own wickedness. But things were as they were and he had to survive, and surviving meant he had to get through his existence as well as he could. He must stand up for himself. So in conclusion, he decided his purpose in life was to look after Sheila. Anything else he did that was good or bad didn't matter to him as long as he fulfilled that task. This would be the focus of his life from now on.

He moved forward with this new sense of purpose and felt a warmth towards Sheila he had never felt before; it was a sacrificial and unconditional love.

Over the following few days, the Aurora Borealis and Aurora Australis displayed their mystery and beauty before the eyes of every nation. Astronauts in space were instructed to avoid spacewalks until the geomagnetic storms had passed. Long distance radio communication was drastically effected and millions of people throughout the world were victim to power cuts.

Everyone who looked upon and considered the beauty and majesty of these events spent time soul-searching.

China

All across China, millions watched the night skies to witness the colourful displays. Artists and authors were inspired by the beauty and romance of the phenomenon, and would later create poetry and stories to be read by many in the future, literature that would survive into the next era.

Many of the peculiar disasters such as floods, disease, drought and famine had fled from the huge nation.

This was a time of soul-searching for Zhang Lili who had struggled with her conscience during the famine as she had looked upon emaciated bodies throughout her city, dead or dying in the dirt, while she and her family had had enough 'guanxi' for reasonable health.

She thought to herself, 'There must be more to life than a mixture of joy, sadness, life and death.' She began to wonder what actually happened to people after they had died. She couldn't imagine just ceasing to exist and she couldn't imagine there being ghosts walking invisibly and miserably throughout the world either. She couldn't imagine people being reborn as another person because the world's population had reduced drastically in recent years. 'There must be another answer!' she thought. Was it realistic to consider a human spirit just floating around the universe waiting until another baby came into existence? And if she came back as an animal, what would happen to her personality, the person she was at that moment? Nothing seemed to make sense.

She considered finding out more about Chris Carter's beliefs. He had told her that the Holy Bible was the world's best seller, not just a western favourite. The Bible was for everyone in every nation. In that book people would find out the answer to life and how we were all created. He had said that the Bible told you how to live your life in a way that pleased God and how to love even your enemies.

Israel

The Olivers witnessed the Aurora display too, and rather than pondering over the mysteries of life, they felt even more negatively about the future because of their strange son. Seeing the wonders of the universe only compounded their sense of despair over their life.

Christaff was fourteen and a half years old. He was top of his class in both the Arts and the Sciences. However, his creative essays caused his teachers a great deal of concern because of their content. He was clearly disturbed. He was very intelligent but no one could bring themselves to trust him. His character was too secretive and manipulative. All of this, coupled with his intelligence, brought concern over the evil he was capable of, given the right circumstances and position of power.

Two of his teachers vowed to keep a close eye on him over the ensuing years, and if he was to rise to some sort of position of influence, they would do their best to thwart him.

In Jerusalem, temple ceremonies continued. The phenomena in the sky in recent times had given a sense of awe to devout Jews and those designated as Levitical priests. They saw it as a sign of God's presence, and confirmation of his approval of their temple worship.

Outdoors and beside the temple, Prince Jasper led a huge gathering of Jews in giving thanks and praise to the Creator of the universe as they looked up to the skies.

Joanna viewed the Aurora and considered how amazing the universe was. She thought back to God's promise to Abraham's descendants again being as unsearchable as the stars of the universe full of billions of galaxies. To her, the beauty and significance of God's plans for her people was greater than the wonder of the heavenly display above her head. It only reinforced her determination to work on her tapestry and record the unfolding events surrounding her people.

France

Jinny and Frank admired the night time display. It touched Frank's heart to some degree. Although he had been severely depressed over his own existence and puzzled over global events, this one did awaken some hope in his heart and gave him an awareness of a higher power. But in the end, the only difference the Aurora made to his existence was to give him the courage to attempt to return to Britain for good.

This plan was a risk for both of them because France was the safest place for Christians and Jinny had become a Christian. Britain was not as tolerant, but they missed Chris and Michelle, and wanted to see their niece. Jinny also missed her sister Mary.

During the Aurora Jinny saw the light. She firmly believed that God was all-powerful and all-loving. She recommitted herself to her Saviour and pledged to stand by her suffering husband.

*

Pierre, on the outskirts of Paris, sat on a chair in his favourite field, with a flask of beef soup and his trusty shotgun, looking out at the mysterious phenomenon around him. He thought about his wife who had died of cancer when she was only 31. He thought about his two estranged sons who didn't want anything to do with his life and estate. Perhaps when he died they would visit him to claim their inheritance, but until that day, he guessed they would continue to pursue their careers and the high life. He supposed they saw their father as a sad, lonely, out of date and out of touch recluse, but Pierre knew he was worthy of more dignity than that.

Pierre's character was different to his sons'. He honestly felt he had no need of endless fake friendships, jet setting, dinner parties and shady business deals. Yes, he was lonely from time to time, but he was happy with his lot, and life wasn't too complicated; he had no hang-ups, addictions or competitors to distract him. Nature was beautiful and this night proved it. He took a slurp of beef soup and nestled into his seat enjoying the sensation of hot steam sweeping across his face.

England

Lucy Granger saw the lights and it made her think of the highest power of all, something she was unable to supersede, but she quickly dismissed it from her mind and kept her gaze down because it would distract her from her evil cause.

*

Jenny Cartright had clung to a sense of guilt over her husband's death, for a long time; she had been unfaithful to him while he was serving his country in the heat of the Kingdom Battle. She also despaired over the death of the Carters' first baby when her car rammed into the back of the car baby Jasmine had been in. But her life had undergone a change as a consequence. Her uncontrollable pursuit of wealth and power at the expense of others had subsided. But this determination to be a better person didn't bring her more happiness, because she was in a world that didn't recognise conscience as valid. A respectable lifestyle was seen to be naive, foolish, prudish and judgemental. She couldn't find a way to be happy. It was as though the world had everything in reverse. Good was seen as evil and evil was seen as good. Seeing signs in the sky added to her despair as she felt everything was outside of her control, and that didn't fit her personality.

Narrator

Global troubles, trials and tribulations hit again: bang bang bang! What was to be the outcome of this global tapestry under construction, weaving, turning, twining in a multiplicity of colours and fabrics?

Part 8

ADRENALINE RUSH

WATCHERS

The chosen ones throughout the world have noticed how much soul-searching is going on across the globe as a result of the Aurora displays. They are taking the opportunity to tell their neighbours, relatives and friends about the Creator of all these things, calling on them to put their trust in Jesus.

Many people are doing just that, as they are nearing the close of an era. However, most of the peoples of the world have decided to remain ignorant of the fact that this era is coming to an end, so in spite of the global signs and friendly warnings, they continue with their mundane and cyclic road to death.

Meanwhile, King Hassan is ordering the massacre of the Jewish nation. Fallen angels sit inside the despot feeling smug, believing there is a chance of success at this closing of an era.

CHAPTER 23

Signs From Above

A few days had passed after the Aurora displays. Then a new phenomenon hit the skies, witnessed by many nations. It started with an extraordinarily dark sky at night. Even in the countryside, absent of light pollution, there were no visible stars, and then as if by the flick of a switch, the stars came on much brighter than usual. In addition to this, many thousands more stars were suddenly visible to the naked eye, and they all appeared larger and brighter. The night sky was so bright it became like daytime with an unusual and mysterious colourful backdrop. Then to add to the fearful sight, stars danced across the sky, darting to and fro. Some stars seemed to move in swirling formations, making various patterns and lines.

Cameras were out en masse to capture countless images of these things, keeping a pictorial record for the future.

False prophets, including Shep Grifford and Rabbi Nathaniel, capitalised on this and later provided their own phenomena of a similar nature, although only the immediate vicinity above the audiences' heads displayed these things, and there was no physical effect upon stars or space. Nevertheless, many were fooled into a self-gratifying idolatrous worship of fake Messiahs, who said, "All you have to do is follow me and you will earn peace. Do not be depressed and racked with guilt, your redemption is coming here on Earth; do not look to the sky for another. The Messiah is here. Do not look for another to come from the sky, it is just a lie to take away pleasure from your life and peace from your heart."

But their followers were without excuse! The powers of the heavens had been shaken and everyone knew this was the Creator giving warning. So in response to this idolatrous worship of false Christs, the Creator sent a more prolonged darkness that could not be attributed to an eclipse, and with it came a heavy jet black atmosphere that clung to their flesh like a deadly skin disease. They felt insecure and alone, yet they still did not turn away from their evil practices. The genuine signs were intended to inspire repentance, not idolatry.

Making A Splash

Lucy Granger couldn't find out from her spirit guides where the Carters were, no matter how hard she tried. Her spirits were muzzled by a higher authority. For the time being therefore, she decided to link up with Chris' church to see what disturbances she could cause, and also to look for clues as to the Carters' location. Word was, Michelle's parents had no idea either, because Chris and his family had gone into hiding after escaping from the CEC police, and it wasn't safe to contact them.

It wasn't easy getting acquainted with Chris' church as they tended to be more hush hush due to the Cod-eye police, but as long as no one put out an APB on any of them they were relatively okay.

The holy people in Chris' church were a mystery to her as she had limited power over them.

She attended their baptism ceremony at a secret location along the Itchen River and wanted so much to have some impact during the proceedings. In a way she wanted to be a proper member of the group and for her to have that 'unidentified' power and peace that these people had, but instead she was comforted by her familiar lifelong spirit guides with which she felt an affinity. She set them in motion and they disrupted the beautiful occasion. She had a sense that she could not change people's minds in regard to their promises to follow the King of kings and to live a holy life, but she wasn't without some power! The River was calm and the sky sunny, but she changed that. The wind picked up and began to swirl within a dull, grey atmosphere.

Out went the people to be baptised, wading into the cold choppy waters of the River, shivering and shaking with the cold. Lucy heard the words being uttered in the distance as the Minister raised one hand into the sky: "I now baptise you in the name of the Father, the Son and the Holy Spirit." Two men held the shoulders of candidates, and one by one, they allowed them to drop backwards into the water, being completely submerged before they were lifted back out again to the applause of onlookers.

They eventually made their way back to the edge of the River, shivering but smiling as the brethren, friends and family applauded.

Lucy wanted to be part of all this so much that she felt physically sick and couldn't stand it anymore. She hadn't realised it, but she had gradually waded out into the waters during the stormy outbreak she had caused. It was settling down and becoming mild again, but both outside her body and inside her mind, Lucy was feeling oppressed. She felt a sickly stirring and shuffling. Her mind was becoming dull. She began to shake in spite of being comfortable and warm in her extra clothing. Everything around her went blurred and she fell backwards into the water unconscious. Even though she was unconscious, she was flapping her arms around and screeching unidentifiable syllables between clenched teeth and foaming mouth. Eventually, it caught the attention of the chosen ones who rushed to her aid to prevent her from drowning. She was lovingly carried to the side of the River where she eventually came round. The Minister and his wife took her back to their house in their car. As they were driving away from the baptism site the sky became blue again and the wind ceased.

Mr. Harrison

Mr. Harrison returned to England from China and locked his car near his new home on the Norfolk coast. After days of continuous torrential rain, the muddy surrounding to his newly built house didn't stand a chance of sprouting grass for a natural lawn. Set high above a relatively new coastline, the brand new house had a perfect view of the ocean.

He walked along the paving slabs leading up to the house. They had been put down temporarily until the gardens and driveway could be established. Just a few paces away from his side door, the two paving slabs on which he stood started to slide. He looked around and noticed the soily ground was shifting around. All of a sudden, the ground opened up in several places. One split occurred near him, creating a muddy slope leading towards a long, deep and narrow gap. Mr. Harrison slid until he fell vertically downwards. As he fell, the pliable mountain of land readjusted itself, clasping his body tight. His chest was so tightly compressed he couldn't speak. Tiny pockets of air between particles of soil contained life-giving chemicals, and the size of his gasps were just as small as the tiny pockets of air. However, the oxygen was gone in seconds.

Mr Harrison hadn't expected his life to end at this stage and he had barely spent any time in his new house. His life flashed before

191

him, his ups and downs, his good deeds and his bad ones, his loved ones and the ones that hated him. He wondered, 'Was this a complete life? Was this an example of a typical existence? Was it a meaningful stretch?'

There he was, seconds lasting what felt like minutes, wondering if he would escape this tomb of darkness and loneliness. Would someone be able to resuscitate him? It would have to be very quick! He imagined someone trying to give him CPR on the surface of this sodden soil. The ground would be too soft to provide a firm base on which to make the compressions.

He felt the earth shift again. His body moved sidewards. He heard his bones crunch but felt no pain. Then everything was unbearably tight.

Many died that day, including his neighbours to be who would never be.

A Dainty Dish

Later that week, the skies were a dull grey in Bradford and it looked like rain; but there was a slight breeze and it may have been her only opportunity to get the washing dry. Deborah left her baby in the high chair in the kitchen, but she left the chair by the open door so she could watch her while she hung the washing on the line in the back yard of her terraced house.

Hanging out the washing reminded her of an old familiar nursery rhyme, so she sang it to her baby to keep her happy:

'Sing a song of sixpence, a pocket full of rye,
Four and twenty blackbirds baked in a pie.
When the pie was opened, the birds began to sing;
Wasn't that a dainty dish to set before the king!'

Deborah heard the pattering of little feet and stopped singing. After a moment, she continued while her baby kicked her legs in the high chair giving Deborah a big smile:

'The king was in the counting house, counting out his money;
The queen was in the parlour, eating bread and honey.
The maid was in the garden ... '

She was distracted by the pattering of little feet again and looked around. No one was in sight. Listening and singing at the same time, she continued:

'The maid was in the garden hanging out the clothes, when down came a ... '

Suddenly a fox jumped over the wall, looked around and then leapt up at Deborah who fell backwards in surprise. Her baby screamed as the fox poked and tore at her mother.

259 foxes rampaged through the Bradford housing estate, like orange and red flames darting back and forth, up and over. They entered the local Primary School playground, attracted by the playful screaming. Legs were gripped and yanked by savage and vicious teeth. Children who had already been rendered unconscious were being ripped apart by five or six foxes at a time.

In the nearby streets, toddlers in pushchairs were vulnerable to attack. These orange dogs jumped for their faces while mothers screamed at the foxes and tried to pull the pushchairs away from the predators.

Back in the yard, Deborah had been left splayed across the yard and her baby was missing. A magpie flew down and pecked off Deborah's nose. It flew away with her nose in its beak and rested on a wall nearby, banging and shaking the tasty morsel making it tender enough to swallow and digest.

WATCHERS

Many people still haven't grasped the significance of recent years. The message has been presented to every human being on planet Earth, and people have witnessed many frequent and intensifying pressures to wake them up. Even the Earth itself groans under the strain. They have had their chance, it won't be long before this era closes and a new one begins.

CHAPTER 24

Surficide

The Norfolk and Suffolk coast had received a battering over recent weeks and the waves were colossal. The relatively new surfing society Surficide had made a pact to challenge the elements at their worst, for the greatest thrill of their lives. They began to gather on the east coast and kept up to date with weather forecasts, although they had been unreliable for a long time. When sufficient candidates had gathered at the camp site, they planned their first day.

Because this was potentially going to be a suicide mission, some suggested they write notes and electronic messages to be accessed in case of fatalities. This was going to be the surf of all surfs and there was no turning back, even if it cost them their lives. Soon the group of fifty adrenaline junkies became a hundred.

*

Jinny and Frank embarked upon their ferry journey across the English Channel from Calais to Dover. It was a particularly choppy day, but not bad enough to cancel the voyage. The forecasts were also reasonably good, so they boarded with only a little apprehension. Their cabin was comfortable and they thought they would try to snooze their way across to England.

*

"Let's get out to the beach now, the wind's picking up," said Venessa.

"Okay, who's ready? Are we going for it or not?"

"Wait up, just going for a ......"

"Me too."

"What! You're not nervous are you?"

"No of course not!"

"Why not, I am."

"Right, let's go."

The Surficide group headed for the beach.   Gaz, Jock and
Venessa were well ahead and paddled out into the emerging sea
monster under a darkening sky. Things soon got rough. Many of
the hundred or so adrenaline junkies were unable to get out to sea
far enough. "We need to get as far out as possible, otherwise it'll
be a waste of time," called Jock.

*

Meanwhile, in the ferry, Jinny and Frank were unable to rest as
the boat was rocking to and fro and things were becoming
increasingly uncomfortable.   The wind outside was becoming
louder and stronger.   The captain continued to drive the best he
could, but the engine was stretched to capacity. He knew that if the
ferry broke up, the lifeboats wouldn't stand the knocks either. A
thousand lives were at stake and he was responsible for their safety.
Then a scream came from a crew member, "STARBOARD
SIDE!"   The crew looked over to see what had been invisible
before in the mist, a mountainous wave larger than anyone had
witnessed before. Some passengers were like a random handful of
sand being thrown into the vast ocean by a child. The particles
would disappear and become irretrievable in the raging wind and
waves.
   A directive for everyone to wear life jackets was issued, so Jinny
and Frank complied. They could barely see out of the window, but
what they could see terrified them.   They stared out at the bulging
and looming mass of dark purple water charging at them. Before it
reached them, they felt themselves tilting backwards. The central
bedside table leant against their legs. The beds however remained
still and they guessed they were fixed to the floor, so they quickly
jumped onto their respective beds, clinging on tightly to the
headboards. The covers slid off from beneath them as the boat
seemed to tilt endlessly.   Then they felt a surge beneath them
making them rise up. They glanced out of the window to see the
ocean beneath them as though they were on the Dubai Tower
looking down. Then the ferry was flung downwards, tilting in the
other direction.   Frank's head banged against the wall, but
unfortunately it didn't render him unconscious. The next thing was
the sight of whirl winds on the sea horizon. With this sight came a

196

whirlpool as big as a city. The water dipped downwards into a cone-shape and the ferry began to soar and spin. The lights went out and Jinny and Frank closed their eyes. Jinny cried out to God to save them and the hundreds of passengers.

*

The highest waves the surfers had ever seen were bashing the Norfolk coast, and the surfers got more than they bargained for. They were right to leave notes and messages for their families and friends.

Gaz, Jock and Venessa had managed to get a long way out to where the huge waves were building up. All three of them popped. The adrenaline rushed through their whole being; this was the greatest thrill of their lives, one they were willing to die for. Jock managed to catch sight of Venessa. She looked a little unsteady but she was holding her own. Venessa was soaking up the experience. At the back of her mind she held memories of her parents' divorce and how that had devastated her. She had become more independent though, which she thought was a good thing. She thought of people who had influenced her life and remembered the good and the bad experiences. She thought of the few potential Mr. Rights and how they had failed her. These waves were now her lover. She gave her heart and soul to the waves. Jock did the same. He liked Venessa, but nothing compared to this. The thrill dominated every emotion in his heart, but he felt some regret at his decision to ride the waves that day; he suspected it would kill him or at least paralyse him. He debated whether this one experience was worth it but he knew it was too late to turn back, so he made the most of it. He screamed and yelled in delight. The sound of the roaring waves was so powerful that his voice was inaudible. To top it all, he could see meteors in the darkened sky, not evaporating, but falling into the sea around him, orange flames splashing into the waves releasing steam into the air as they hit the surface. It was more than awesome, it was the ride of his life, the greatest ever adrenaline rush, the best ever suicide mission.

Others popped, but most of the surfers had already died in the swirling currents. The ocean decided to claim more land on the coast. The tide began to grab the cliffs, soaking them and making them crumble.

*

Meanwhile, Jinny and Frank couldn't believe the speed at which the elements abated. Their ferry began to stop spinning and as the storm began to settle they could hear other passengers' voices more distinctly. They were reassuring voices although each one had a tone of panic and sheer unbelief. After quarter of an hour of witnessing a settling down, people began to pop their heads out of their cabin doors to see soaking and exhausted crew members walking up and down reassuring passengers and urging them to stay indoors as they were still on course and they had no need to worry. They were told it was too dangerous to go on deck though in case the storm returned.

*

Things were still rough for the surfers and that was how they wanted it, but they did not expect the tide to go inland so much that the beach was swallowed up. As the only surfers left breathing, five thrill seekers surfed towards the Norfolk cliffs for the last time. Ahead of them they saw the brown soil of the cliffs crumbling and collapsing into the sea. What they could not see was the occasional dead and decomposing victims of a mudslide being released into the crashing waves. Along with them the mangled body of Mr. Harrison was partially released and left dangling from the muddy, vertical face, waiting to greet the surfers on their death mission. Gaz, Jock and two others were pummeled between the cliff face and the force of the waters. At the same time, Venessa went flying up and over the cliff edge onto land, a sole survivor.

Angels

Meanwhile, in the south of England, Chris woke up with a start, and the angels surrounding him, those that had been given paramount responsibility for his welfare, arose immediately. They got to work on protecting and watching his family, clearing the way ahead. Some looked outside for potential spiritual attack; they had swords. One was close at hand to keep the three of them in reasonable health. Two watched over their intentions and decisions, tweaking them if necessary and organising the road ahead; this family was important for the future during these difficult times.

Weeks had passed since the Carters had gone into hiding and they were wondering whether it was time to make contact with their respective parents and relatives. They guessed that if the CEC police were still looking for them, they would have found them by now or someone would have phoned to warn them. As it was they had received no calls so everyone was still protecting their whereabouts and didn't want the calls to be traced. Having said that, as far as they knew, Michelle's parents were the only ones who knew their location. They temporarily carried on living in secrecy until there was a good enough reason to risk getting in contact.

The ministering spirits, the Creator's angels, helped them with this decision as the family were unaware of Chris' parents' involvement and how his sisters would blame Chris and Michelle for their parents' demise if they were to contact them.

The Silenced Storm

Back in Norfolk, the storm abated as quickly as it had begun and Venessa limped in agony towards a nearby hamlet in her wet suit thanking God that she had survived. Her heart was still pumping with excitement, and with every palpitation came a searing pain across her chest. She crumpled to the floor laughing hysterically and in agony at the same time; this broke into sobs as she grieved over the loss of her companions. Then, under the dull but clearing skies she saw several figures between her and the hamlet. She got up and attempted to focus as she hobbled forward. They wore grey and looked a bit peculiar. They looked towards her with some curiosity. To Venessa their faces were odd and the size of their heads too large. They were wearing clothes so were surely people? It was difficult to focus, but their faces looked a little bit like the faces of bulls. She kept blinking to clear her vision and wondered if she was hallucinating; they remained a while longer, and then all of a sudden she couldn't see them anymore. Her pounding heart skipped a beat and then continued to thump through her chest. She couldn't remember being able to hear her own heart so loudly before, not without a stethoscope anyway. Even her limping was interrupted by the throbbing of that organic machine within her body, moving her physical frame back and forth.

WATCHERS

At this stage of rebellion and lack of faith throughout the world, demons are gaining opportunities to possess and oppress more and more people. Armies of holy angels regularly gather together, especially at the request of the Creator's chosen ones. These deliverers are radiant and effective in their fight. The Beast and the Dragon act in their own interests, but the prayers of the chosen ones will prevail against the will of the Dragon.

CHAPTER 25

Heroes and Heroines

Venessa finally reached one of the houses. It had stood out from a distance when she was thrown onto land because there were lots of electric lights on in and around the house. As she approached the front door across the garden, she had to avert her eyes from the garden spotlight. She pulled an old fashioned bell beside a pristine yet old fashioned door. A smiling old man and woman came to the door. "Oh deary me, come in sweety. What happened?"

Venessa told them of her wonderful experience and how she now had to face the consequences. But even though she was in a lot of pain, she did not regret it one little bit. The woman said, "You know it was a very silly thing to do, don't you deary?"

"Yes I know it was, I've learnt from my mistake now, I'll never do it again," she said, not meaning a word of it. She thought they were a weird old couple, but sweet. She decided to play along for a while because she was seriously injured and they might even give her a bit of food or even some cash. So Venessa played the childlike victim, not even sure the old couple were falling for it or not. 'They are behaving like I'm their long lost daughter, or the daughter they never had,' thought Venessa. "Er, may I use your bathroom please?" she asked.

"Yes of course sweety, it's just at the top of the stairs on the landing. Second door on the left."

"Thank you," said Venessa with a childlike grin.

At the top of the stairs she couldn't find the bathroom, and walking to the end of the corridor she noticed a small staircase going down the other side of the house.

At the bottom of the staircase was a small wooden door. She wondered if that was the bathroom. The rest of the house was posh, but this was definitely not a posh door.

Trying the door handle, it didn't budge at all. It was locked. There were slight gaps between wooden slats in the door and a draught blew against her face. With the draught came a terrible stink. "It must be the most filthy bathroom in England!" she said quietly to herself. At that moment she heard some shuffling behind her, felt a heavy thud on her head and then passed out.

When Jinny and Frank emerged from their cabin and onto the deck, they couldn't believe their eyes. How anyone had survived this they did not know? The cars remaining on the ferry were strewn across the deck like toy cars that had been abandoned by a child. As they disembarked, they saw Royal Navy helicopters receiving wounded passengers.

They later discovered only twenty-one people had been claimed by the waves and seventy-nine were taken to various hospitals.

*

Venessa came round, her skin feeling cold and damp; the atmosphere in the room was clammy and a stench filled her nostrils. She opened her eyes to see rancid clumps of raw flesh all over the floor, and sharp metallic objects on tables and dangling from the ceiling. Amongst them were hooks of various sizes. In the room with her were two men, the old man who had greeted her at the door, and a younger man with a moustache. They had shabby looking clothes on as though they were doing some dirty work. Their clothing was stained with browns and dark red smudges, but the most dominant sensation she was experiencing was the stench of rotten flesh. As her mind became more focused she realised these people were butchers and it was clearly not animals they were in the habit of butchering. She was to be the next carcass. 'Are they going to butcher me alive or dead?' she wondered. Then in a rush, all of her survival instincts came to the fore. She was not going to survive the most dangerous surf in history to be chopped up by a couple of perverted cannibals! She imagined all the things she was willing to do to these sickos in her process of escape while her mind quickly assessed her predicament.

Venessa decided it was time for action. Her wrists were tethered with leather, one arm attached to a metal pipe and one to a shackle fastened securely into a wall. Even if she somehow got her hands free, she had one foot manacled to a heavy cuboid slab of concrete on the floor. She was a goner to any logical mind, but she had survived the most incredible experience ever, and she could not accept that she was simply to be pummelled and torn apart by these monsters.

The two men came towards her having made some decision together, exactly what, she didn't dare to consider. They released her hands and foot, lifted her like a slab of meat and slung her onto a putrid wooden table onto her back. She screamed and grappled for something to attack them with. All her hands could settle on was a loose metal edging on the rim of the table. It had obviously lost some screws, but one or two were still trying to stay in place. She wiggled and pulled at the metal object unnoticed while she was pinned onto her back. It worked free. She lifted her hand into the air holding the broken, rusty metallic object, and stabbed at one of her attackers with all the strength she could muster. The object shot clean through the young man's eye and into his brain. She couldn't believe what a natural aim she had. Blood seeped out as he collapsed onto the floor, a youthful death. The old man was dumbfounded and reached for one of the cleavers on a small table behind him.

Venessa wondered whether this was one potential victory too far. After escaping a surf-tide of death, and being untethered just long enough to kill one assailant in this house of horrors, how could she expect to be lucky enough to defeat this last monster; and then she would also have the task of getting out of the house and past Grendel's mother.

She quickly psyched herself up, and felt ready to chop off the creature's head. In sheer agony, she mustered enough power to get off the table and face her attacker. However, he leapt at her, brandishing the cleaver. She ducked as he swung it at her head. A sharp pain in her chest winded her, but she managed to lunge for a meat hook on the floor.

"Come here you little upstart!" breathed the fiery oppressor. "I'm going to slice you into little pieces. COME HERE!"

Venessa swung the meat hook at him as she tried to get back onto her feet. She aimed for his torso, but it only reached as far as his knee cap. He let out an agonising yelp as he clenched his knee and removed the hook. "Take that you creep!" she yelled. The evil enemy's posture made him vulnerable to further attack, and Venessa wasn't going to miss her opportunity. Finding a heavy, rusty old chain, she ran up behind him and thrashed him across his back. "Arghhh!" the man screamed. She beat him with the chain until he fell to the floor on his side. She decided to finish the job. Seeing the hook he had removed from his knee, she picked it up and lunged at his neck with the clumsy weapon. The sharp point of the hook wasn't coming into direct contact with his flesh, so she kept trying to change the angle of the thrusts. Eventually it made an impact. She then pulled it out of his neck, bringing with it some of his flesh and sinews. She crouched and thrust the point into his neck again. This time blood poured out as she yanked it back out. She stuck it into his neck again and left it there, hoping that would finish the job.

Managing to get back onto her feet, she headed towards a staircase. At the top of the staircase was a wooden door. She guessed it was probably the same door she had been stood next to before she was knocked unconscious.

She stumbled up the stairs, and emerging from the stench, clambered out onto the landing and looked over the balcony, down at the evil old lady in her rocking chair. She was knitting something for who knows what. Venessa now had to decide whether she was going to destroy that creature too. She felt like a murderess although technically she had only acted in self defence.

After creeping downstairs with her fists ready to beat her up, she tiptoed behind the back of the rocking chair, and the old woman croaked, "Albert, is that you? Did you put the oven on like I told you? It needs to be nice and hot before you cook her. We want a good roast this time!"

Feeling bashed, beaten and bold she walked round to face the old woman with sneering disgust. The old woman jerked back in surprise. "Now then pretty one, where is my husband AND MY SON! Have you used your feminine charms on him?"

Sarcastically, Venessa said, "They have left us and gone to a better place. Actually, they decided to leave you, you sick old witch. Want to cook me do you?"

"You don't understand people like me; we belong to a higher order. You are just a skimpy little flirt."

Venessa felt such power on her side; she was a victim of kidnappers, violent and evil murderers, and she had survived the most incredible surf ever. Surely she had the right to squeeze that scrawny neck!

But she couldn't. That would make her a murderess and she would only be hurting herself. Instead she uttered a curse: "May your scrawny little neck snap the next time you step out of this house of torture. You're an evil, sadistic psychopath and you don't deserve to breathe. I'm leaving now, and don't you even think of getting out of that rocking chair or you will end up in that cellar with a meat hook under your chinny chin chin."

She headed towards the door, glancing back every so often in case the old woman followed her. She panicked momentarily when she saw bolts across the front door, but she managed to open them and get out.

Two young men called Tony and Josh were walking in the early evening, wondering if any more bodies were going to be found and whether the serial killer or killers would be found. They had walking sticks, which were actually weapons in disguise in case they came across any serial killers. Ahead of them, they saw an attractive young woman. Tony nudged Josh saying, "I think I've just died and gone to Heaven, just look at that!"

"Wow, I'm in love," said Josh, who then shouted over to her, "Will you marry me?"

Limping, Venessa casually replied, "Are you really sure? I've already killed two men."

Guessing she was joking, Tony said, "You've already killed me!"

Josh finally noticed she was limping and said, "Hey, you're hurt! What happened?"

"Took you a while to notice!" exclaimed Venessa. Venessa was in desperate need of food and water as her energy levels were zero, and she suspected she was dehydrated too. She was inclined to trust these two normal looking guys; they were after all no different to her surfing buddies. So, with this acknowledgement, her body relinquished the need for another top up of adrenaline. The young men saw her collapse and ran enthusiastically to her rescue.

*

Later that evening, the old woman left her house by the back door in search for a saw, because wielding the cleavers would require a lot of strength. She thought a saw would make it a bit easier for her to cut up the bodies of her husband and son. Cutting up the bodies would also make it easier to dispose of them. She had no choice as little madam may tell the authorities who would then come looking. Seeing the dead bodies of her husband and son would only confirm her story.

Between the back door and her shed, a sudden gust of wind knocked the old woman off her feet. As she fell, her neck banged against the frame of an old rusty metal chair which was leant against the shed. She felt excruciating pain and heard a snap. Ending up on her back and paralysed by the blow, she choked on her own blood.

*

Venessa awoke to see and hear one of the young men, Josh, reading out loud from the Bible. It was as though he was reading her the last rites! Josh and Tony had taken her to the local cottage hospital where the staff had fixed her up as well as they could. They had put a splint on her leg and had discovered she had several fractured ribs. She was also very bruised and on pain killing drugs.

Venessa struggled to speak because of the pain, but she managed to share her experiences with her two new companions. They were amazed and would not have believed all of it if they hadn't been aware of the existence of a serial killer in the first place. Josh told her there had been a lot of gruesome murders around that area for months and they had hoped to catch the culprit themselves, but it looked like she had found them and dealt with them already. They told her that people were finding body after body all over the nearby villages; sometimes the bodies were already badly decomposed because they had been murdered weeks before. The state of these bodies was apparently unbearable to look at. They personally hadn't found any, but they had spoken to people who had. Some of the victims had body parts missing too. "So, it looks like you killed the psychos, except for the old witch of course. So, when you're better you can show us where she lives and we will keep an eye on her," suggested Tony.

"I don't think you'll have much trouble with her, she's too old and weak, but I suppose it's worth watching the house anyway," said

Venessa adding, "So, thank you for saving me guys, you are my little heroes."

"I think you're the hero, a real life psycho slayer!" said Josh.

"I've never been a hero before, a heroine I mean; I am a girl after all."

"You're certainly one of those!" said Tony.

WATCHERS

The nations are in distress and perplexed because of the roaring of the sea and the waves amongst all the other strange events; people are frequently fainting with fear and foreboding at what is coming on the world. Humankind feels out of control. They can't stop tragic events occurring and there is nowhere safe to flee to.

CHAPTER 26

Sheer Fear

Jinny and Frank used Michelle's parents' home as a stop gap again, and although they were looked after, it was all too much for Frank. The sheer fear in both his heart and mind at the stirring and tossing of the sea! People were being ripped apart by animals going berserk, and earthquakes were striking everywhere; he couldn't cope with it all any longer! He had been sat on the sofa unable to control his body tremors, his mind still believing he was on the ferry, tossing around on the giant, mountainous waves; up and down, up and down; then in the whirlpool, round and round, dipping down towards the abyss.

It was all beyond his ability to endure. His mind could not lift itself out of its pit of fear. Jinny entered the living room and noticed he was no longer on the sofa. Where could he be? She went outside to see if he was in the garden. This was something he had done on several occasions in France during his bad nights.

But instead, Frank was at the top of the stairs, feeling like he was on top of a gigantic wave about to be engulfed by a mountainous barrage of heaviness. He gazed through the wall ahead of him as though it was his cabin window, towards an imaginary monstrous purple and blue wave. He stopped breathing. While still standing, his body spun and flew backwards down the stairs, his head clattering as he descended.

Jinny heard the sound and went rushing in to see what was happening, only to find her husband had fallen head first down the stairs, his empty eyes looking up at her. Cradling him and calling for help, she knew his life had ended. In some ways she felt a sense of relief on his behalf.

Three watching angels remained at her side, viewing her responses and assessing her state of mind. They knew she would be okay, but would help her in the coming days.

*

Meanwhile, Josh's church was having a social outing. It included Josh and his friends, three families with children and a few others.

They had a picnic and games organised on the sea front, and Josh promised to help with looking after the kids. Venessa joined Josh, Tony and the others, and was impressed with how close they all were, and how much they cared about each other.

After the food and a few games, there was a commotion beside some nearby chalets that weren't being used. Suzy, a little girl of three, had been jumping around and exploring when she was found screaming in terror after seeing inside a chalet room through an open door. She stamped her little legs up and down in sheer horror after seeing something no one else had seen. She had found one of the dead victims of the now deceased serial killers. One of the grandmothers grabbed the little child without looking at the horrible sight, but dried blood was visible on the floor, having previously seeped from the open doorway.

Tony hugged the little girl, trying to imagine how traumatic it must have been. Josh also wanted to help this child to overcome her shock as much as possible, not only then but also in the future, as he knew it would take a long time for the little girl to get over it. He decided the only way he could do that was to see exactly what she saw. He asked Tony to keep hold of her for a moment while he apprehensively crept towards the doorway. Josh couldn't bear the thought of it, but he had to do it. How else could he help the child unless he could understand what she was trying to describe in the future? Venessa tried to pull him back, but he insisted. So instead, she just kept hold of his arm to provide him with a feeling of support and in case he fainted with shock.

At the door frame, Josh gradually tilted his head to the side to take in the view. His stomach churned as he did so; his legs turned to jelly and his head went dizzy. What he saw was beyond adequate description. A precious human being had been almost unfolded, with threads of skin holding onto random bones and limbs. The body's eyes were at either end of the extended mass of ripped flesh. It was as though the mass of skin, bone and blood had been carefully draped from the wardrobe door.

Fixed to the spot, his body and mind froze as he tried to find a way to acknowledge and contain the image of horror. Just like an electrocuted hand involuntarily grips a live wire, so his body became immobile. But two ministering spirits nudged his body away sufficiently for him to escape the image and regain mobility.

Lord Trigalon

In a secret location, east of Israel, an abominable object of false worship was being developed. It was being made from a variety of materials, fluorescent and colourful. It was given the name 'Lord Trigalon'. The name Trigalon sounded remarkably like Jabulon, an object of worship endorsed by Free Masons for similar reasons of combining a variety of gods into one focus of worship. In this case however, 'Tri' represented the Trinity of the Christians and the three-headed god of the Hindus, 'Al' represented Allah of the Muslims, their name for God.

This was seen as sufficient for the Jews too as 'Allah' was from the Arabic language and Arabic was in the same linguistic family as Hebrew. The word 'Lord' was seen as a fair compromise too, as Jews refused to pronounce the name of their God anyway, referring to him as 'Adonai', meaning 'Lord'.

The statue's form and appearance was also significant. It was sat in the lotus position, representing many statues of Buddha, with a big open mouth into which would go everyone's sins or unhappiness; it had breasts representing the sensuality of many modern religious beliefs and the nurture of new life. Two snakes were wrapped around the body of the statue symbolising power related to many ancient and modern practices. It sat on a bed of leaves out of respect for nature gods, and its head looked like a cross between a bull and a goat, acceptable to many pagan traditions and various forms of witchcraft. It had two arms, one raised to Heaven and one pointing towards the Underworld, connecting the two.

After construction, it would be used in an attempt to unite all religions and religious practices.

Part 9

THE END OF AN ERA

CHAPTER 27

The Exodus

News Report

'Tectonic plate activity is more pronounced than ever. With the added complexity of climate change and unexpected changes in our solar system, the effects of disturbances within the Earth's crust are intensified. There are countless areas ready to break and old volcanoes are smoking and becoming active again. The oceans and tides are frequently disturbed and unpredictable. It is also increasingly difficult for marine biologists to do effective and accurate research. Many marine species are under threat of extinction too, and large water mammals are washed up and stranded on beaches and shores in their thousands.

'These disasters have been referred to as part of what has been called the Great Tribulation, a phrase actually taken from the Holy Bible. Many religious fundamentalists have been using this phrase to persuade people to follow their beliefs. Most of these groups predict that the Creator of the universe will send his Son to rescue his disciples from these worldwide disasters. They claim every person on Earth will see the Son in the sky and he will send out his angels to collect the chosen ones.

'We are now going over to Jim Barley, our correspondent in Israel. Jim, is this religious fundamentalism a serious problem in the Middle East at the moment?'

'Indeed it is. Many such fundamentalists proclaim this message and the general populace in the Middle East see this as a hindrance to religious equality. Although most see the fundamentalists as morally and intellectually weak, and intellectual ones simply a freak of nature, they are still considered to be a threat to stability in the region. These fanatics are breaking international law which states: 'If anyone holds a religious or political view that deliberately counters or contradicts another, that person or persons should incur the penalty of incrimination, the greatest and most likely penalty being human execution."

'So have the Middle-Eastern authorities found a solution to this crisis?'

'Yes, the World Religious Affairs Committee has decided that the Jewish temple should not only be available to the Jews, but any religious group, whether it be Christians, Jews, Muslims, Witches, Druids, worshippers of local Christs, Buddhists, Hindus and people from a variety of minority religions.

'It is believed that people from all over the world and from every religious persuasion, should be granted easier access to Jerusalem the holy city. It is one of the busiest cities in the world as far as religious adherents are concerned, so religious equality and religious commercialism in the area is essential.

'To facilitate this unity, an object or focus of worship representing all religious beliefs is to be set up. In spite of opposition, it was decided that religious equality could be facilitated by enlisting advice from a working group of devout and learned scholars representing diverse religious backgrounds. They have created an image made from a variety of materials and symbolising all faiths. This will be placed within the sanctuary of the temple in Jerusalem. This object of worship has been designed to incorporate as much of every religion as possible and to cater for all beliefs in harmony, and anyone who opposes this 'harmony' should clearly be seen as 'discordant' and liable to discipline or death.'

'That sounds very good Jim, but are protests against this move expected in Jerusalem?'

'The World Religious Affairs Committee is hoping for a peaceful and even glorious atmosphere as the Lord Trigalon is delivered to the temple. Dignitaries from the Committee's representative countries will be present and as one would expect, the United Nations has provided a peace keeping force at the Committee's request as unrest is a possibility. The UN has also been granted permission to shoot to kill any antagonists.'

'Let's hope this force isn't necessary and that the religious zealots and fundamentalists will see sense and seize this as an opportunity for not only lasting peace in the Middle East, but also as a wonderful and harmonious religious experience.'

'But, how is this going to work in practice? Aren't there going to be too many people trying to get into the temple at the same time? And surely everyone will have their own unique way of worshipping. How will these issues be addressed?'

'There are still consultations in regard to what form of religious

practice is to be permitted within the confines of the temple itself....'

Resentment and Bitterness

Michelle's mother, Mary, knew they had to wait at least a month before they communicated with her daughter, son-in-law and granddaughter while they were in hiding, in case their calls were traced. But they wondered if the death of Michelle's uncle was enough justification for taking a risk. Michelle would probably want to know. So Mary picked up the phone and called. Chris answered the phone, and was then left with the job of breaking the news to his wife, which was no easy task as she was already feeling bitter. When he told her she shouted at him, "Why would a loving God do this? Haven't we all suffered enough! I thought God was supposed to love everyone!"

"He does," said Chris. "I don't fully understand why all these things keep happening, but suffering is somehow linked with the fact that we are all sinful. Suffering comes to everyone. I know, I struggle with the issue of evil and suffering myself. I'm sorry, I don't have an answer, but one thing I do know, I trust God even though I don't understand."

"Don't give me all that rubbish!" said Michelle, throwing a dirty cup into the kitchen sink.

After an awkward silence, Michelle added, "Well, someone hates us, because you have to be singled out for some reason before they come and get you, otherwise the CEC police usually leave you alone."

"At least we know we're safe here with our friends," said Chris, trying to reassure her.

Michelle added, "Yes, but it's only a matter of time before they get us. Do you realise I can't even go to the funeral!"

"That's not my fault, it's those wicked Cod-eye police!"

Michelle tried to hold back the tears, "Who do you think betrayed us anyway?"

"I've no idea," replied Chris honestly, still unaware of his parents' betrayal and ensuing execution.

*

219

'Lord Trigalon' arrived in Jerusalem to the cheers of countless thousands of people from all over the world. Many in and around Jerusalem felt this was the final straw. Everyone who disagreed with this event was going to be executed. Their temple was going to be ruined. Everything that had been established since the opening ceremony was now null and void. They could no longer worship at the temple.

The Jewish people fled for their lives, but they did this as secretly as possible. They fled to mountainous regions without turning back for their possessions. The problem was, many of the authorities had already earmarked certain families for execution. Some of their homes were being watched and it would only take their enemies to notice they did not enter into the celebration for them to be confronted and accused of being bigoted. It would then only be a matter of time before they were executed.

During their exodus, it was particularly difficult for pregnant women, those with young children, the sick and the elderly, as they didn't have a guarantee of medical support or hygienic conditions in which to live if they left the area. Many chose not to travel by public transport as they would have to give their ID numbers. So the process of fleeing was traumatic, as they feared for their lives at every turn.

Many well-wishers opened their homes on the way, but this wasn't very effective as the Jews didn't know who they could trust. They couldn't even trust the UN peace keeping force to protect their rights. So, many thousands fled to safety with an uncertain future.

Christaff and his family fled too. Christaff was now 15 years old. He thought it was all hilarious and he watched the events unfold around him with an enthusiastic smile. He knew he had some future major role in the area of politics and religion and he thought this was all good training.

Brother and sister, Sam and Joanna, took their friend Mark with their family as they fled the tensions in Jerusalem and its surrounding areas. This all distressed Joanna and Sam very much and they wondered what the outcome was going to be. It reminded them of the history of their people and in a way it strengthened their faith in their divine heritage.

Amongst the Jews were many others who sympathised with their plight. They were a fly in the ointment to some of the Jews who didn't trust them, but to others they were a comfort. These servants called on the Creator on behalf of the Jews and their prayers seemed to be answered.

After thousands of Jews had settled uncomfortably in the mountains, a story was spread that a mighty deliverance had taken place at Mount Carmel, not dissimilar to the deliverance of Israel from Egypt thousands of years before. In and around Mount Carmel was a secret base for King Hassan's troops where weaponry had been prepared to be used against the convoys of Jews heading in that direction.

But a group of chosen ones gathered in a huddle and prayed for the Creator of all things to destroy the mountain and its weapons and military. It literally happened. People didn't know whether it was an earthquake or the result of a weakening Earth's crust, but the northwestern end of the Carmel mountain range collapsed and slid into the sea. The rumbling could be heard everywhere, but there were no aftershocks typical of earthquakes. And after that event, the convoy had a clear path to the east of the devastated areas.

Mark, Sam and Joanna were however part of the same convoy as Christaff Oliver, and were camped out in the same location as the Oliver family. Mark couldn't quite fathom why this boy had a permanent grin on his face, especially when his parents were suffering with exhaustion and everyone else in the group was flagging under the pressure, despairing of life itself.

Further to the east, one of the smaller convoys was ordered to stop by King Hassan's men. The Jewish exiles were then forced to watch as the soldiers started to execute hand-picked individuals. But one such individual was a catalyst for the convoy's deliverance. A member of the convoy called Simon Eichmann was selected. The executioner grabbed him with some difficulty as Simon was very sturdy and muscular. He also didn't give his executioner the satisfaction of seeing fear in his eyes. He moved with the executioner to the ditch into which all eyes were forced to look. The soldier wanted to handle him like a rag doll but the aggressor looked comical as his own body wriggled and struggled to manoeuvre his victim.

Eventually, Simon was in the location the executioner wanted, stood in blood that had drained from another executed body. Simon didn't bow his head in shame and fear, but instead kept his shoulders straight in a dignified manner. Nevertheless, the soldier who was smaller than him pointed his sword at Simon's neck. He then swung the sword back, before slashing it forward again, severing Simon's head from his body. The decapitated body fell to its knees. The executioner looked up at the mourning onlookers with victorious glee on his face.

But then he noticed that the expressions on the faces in the crowd change. He didn't know what that meant until he looked to where the victim had fallen; he was shocked to see Simon Eichmann's body standing in front of him with his head back on his shoulders.

The soldier fell back and immediately died. The other soldiers ran for their lives while the crowd cheered in sheer unbelief at the miracle that had taken place before their eyes.

*

Ironically, the fact that the Jews fled made the nations despise them all the more, as they were seen as prejudiced against the rest of the world. There was no sympathy for their religious convictions, and the nations watched with approval as 'Lord Trigalon' was wheeled ceremonially into the temple sanctuary.

WATCHERS

The Jews have fled, which is essential for their survival. This is not the first or the last time. From now on, they will be safe as a nation, and the Creator has not abandoned them.

Complacency is out of the question. The stakes are at their highest and people are aware that the consequences are dire, even if they don't know exactly what is coming.

The Creator is going to bolster the hearts of those who are seeking his help. As a result, they will endure until the end. Their message and warnings will be confirmed by extraordinary miracles.

CHAPTER 28

Wise Mortals

"Lord help me to save these people. There are no emergency services here, please give me the strength of Samson." This was the request the passer-by made to the Creator of all things. He was imbued with power from above to help those caught in the traffic accident. He ran to the scene of the crash and the flaming cars. He picked up the burning vehicles from which people had fled and threw them aside to gain access to the screaming family in the crumpled red mass barely recognisable as a vehicle. An elderly woman, two wounded young adults and a mother stood aside in shock as they watched the hero at work. The toddler caught in the wreckage watched in amazement as the hero came to the rescue. "Look Mummy! It's Buperman!" Even in her contorted position beneath the battered roof of her car, she couldn't avoid a painful yet rewarding chuckle.

*

The Minister and his wife cared for Lucy, but she kept quiet the fact that she was part of a secret society attempting to control people like this Minister. She heard that everything she had ever done could be forgiven and suddenly everything began to make sense; her evil lifestyle, however massive it was, became insignificant. She broke down in tears and felt God's loving power around her. But the following days and weeks were difficult. She would often collapse and her limbs would involuntarily thrash around, especially in the most dangerous of places, such as in front of large vehicles, beside water or fire. Her sense of discomfort and agitation would increase whenever she was with the chosen ones. She would daily call out for deliverance from this darkness inside her, as it created a power clash in the presence of the light inside her new companions.

It was a struggle, and she was sick for a while, but evil spirits fled from her body a few at a time, Lucy's body and soul being released little by little. Amongst the many demons that had possessed her, there were twenty very powerful ones. After leaving her body they roamed around seeking new human habitations. These unclean spirits had been in this game for thousands of years. They always chose men and women they hoped they could control and keep away from the King of kings.

*

In Brazil's Rio de Janeiro was a teacher who devoted his time to prayer and self-discipline. His reputation for wise words spread throughout the Americas and beyond. From young to old, pauper to dignitary, all were permitted an audience with him in groups of a hundred. It became conventional to start a question with "Wise man! Wise man! ...."

Each group of one hundred would sit on cushions on the floor of the auditorium for up to two hours at a time. Sunday was the wise man's rest and reflection day. On the other days, questioners' names were put in a box and the teacher would pick out the slips of paper one at a time, and hand them to his assistant who would call out the names. To have your name called out was seen as a blessing as though your question must have international importance.

"Wise man! Wise man! Why is the sky changing?"

"Everything is created in equilibrium, energy is shared, transformed and rebalanced, from the birth of a star at the edge of the universe to the biting of an apple in this room. According to the design of the Creator, this energy naturally never increases or decreases, unless the Creator himself chooses to do otherwise. All energy was created out of nothing and out of nothing he forms new energies as and when the need arises. The Creator can intervene into any universal situation, bringing energy and miraculous power to contradict the natural processes any time he chooses.

"Your question signifies an open heart to question your existence, and my answer is an opportunity to engage with the meaning of life. In producing your heart's inquiry, the Creator is seeking repentance and a sense of responsibility from you. This is what the unexpected events in the sky do, but it is a twofold sword, one that will break the chains binding your heart or one that will condemn you, depending on your response."

*

A family walked along cliffs near the English seaside town of Scarborough. Two children were blown off the edge. Their parents cried out in desperation, but one of the children shouted out to the Creator, who sent two angels to catch the children before they could hit the ground. The angels carried them back up and placed them 200 metres away from the cliff edge. The reunited family returned home in safety and with a story to tell.

*

"Wise man! Wise man! Why are weather forecasts, earthquakes, planetary formations and disease predictions inaccurate?"

"Can you calculate dark matter? Why do you seek stability within the universe, which is secondary to stability within your heart? Is it for the sake of justice that you want to calculate and predict these things? Certainly not! Are the hungry fed? Are the innocent released from prison? For what purpose do you seek answers? Do you want to predict the future so you can get away with murder unnoticed? Do you stand by and let innocents be beaten and crushed? First bring stability to your heart so you can predict justice and righteousness in others, then you will begin to understand the mysteries of life."

"Wise man! Wise man! Why are people becoming more and more evil?"

"What you witness is from the heart of humanity. Universal laws are being broken, and the resulting sense of being out of control shakes forth the thoughts and desires of the heart. World events and the opposing forces at work in the universe are opening the wound, making it visible to all. But in our rebellion we poison ourselves endlessly. We are helpless and hopeless without forgiveness, so we must seek that from our Creator, but people

227

have chosen not to avail themselves of the offer of grace."

*

A doctor on a ward with amputees was getting a bad reputation. He would often pray for his patients and on some occasions new limbs would regrow overnight. Orders for prostheses had often already been made, and these costly items would then become obsolete. Prosthetics companies were threatening to sue the hospital, so the doctor's job was in the balance too as these miraculous signs were deemed unacceptable.

*

"Wise man! Wise man! Are people animals?"

"Humans are made in the image of the Creator, so they are under the spotlight. On the one hand, they are created beings, so have a lower position than their Creator. However, they are also precious, because they are made in the Creator's image, which the animals are not. We know right and wrong and are responsible for our actions. We reap what we sow, animals don't. It is humankind's responsibility to reflect the image of the One who created them. Most people are not reflecting that image and are a blemish to angels and fellow humans."

*

African safaris were still available to those who could afford them, but safety measures left a lot to be desired. On one such occasion, a lion attacked a jeep in Kenya. It tore through the side of the jeep and was lunging at the passengers. It was only because they were huddled up at the other side of the vehicle that the sightseers remained intact. At the back of the jeep was one of the chosen ones called Nigel. He had often told his boss of the substandard safety provisions, but it had fallen on deaf ears.

Nigel called on the Creator and he was given strength and courage to jump out of the jeep, confront the ferocious beast, and tear it limb from limb. Just then a whole pride of lions came rushing towards them. Nigel felt compelled to stretch his arm out in front of him and curse the ferocious and ravenous creatures in God's name. He and his jeep were separated from the pride of lions by a fire that sprung up before their eyes. Everyone, still terrified, considered this to be a lucky coincidence that the hot weather had somehow created a fire. But then it came into perspective when all witnessed a fireball falling from the blue sky and landing on the opposite side of the wall of fire, resulting in screaming wild beasts being engulfed in flames. At that point they realised they were mere mortals under a higher power.

*

"Wise man! Wise man! What exactly should humankind be doing if they are greater than animals like you say?"

"Why are animals going berserk? Animals are part of creation and creation feels the pain of wickedness. The Earth and its creatures were originally created for peace. They cannot cope with the rule of wickedness. They are burdened by the weight of it. But they are not responsible for their own reactions; it is humankind that is responsible for the actions of wildlife. Humankind should nurture and protect the creatures of the animal kingdom, the vegetation of the plant kingdom and the rest of the world's natural resources. These responsibilities are constantly neglected. Earthquakes, disease and disasters are signs and indicators of this neglect and cruelty."

"Wise man! Wise man! Why do humankind not fulfil this responsibility? Is it ignorance, weakness, conditioning, culture or wickedness?"

"We comprise of body, soul and spirit, but the difference between soul and spirit is not yet revealed to us. However, our body is made for our Creator and fellowship with our Creator is the most comfortable fit. Ask yourself why you don't fulfil these responsibilities. You will find the answer in your own corrupt heart."

229

"Wise man! Wise man! People are not wise like you ..."

"I am not wise and you are not wise; wisdom comes from Heaven. But to you, 'ignorance is bliss'."

People started to mutter and complain as he wasn't answering clearly. Yet they were offended at his insinuations! The wise man then added, "In your selfish heart you choose to be ignorant because you think that will absolve you of responsibility."

The questioner was angry. He stood to his feet as the security guards kept close watch. Then he shouted out:

"Have you never heard of looking on the 'bright side of life'? You are so full of doom and gloom. Why don't you have anything positive to say?"

"Haven't recent events told you this is not the season for that? There is a time for joy and laughter, a time for celebration, but now is a time for reflection and administration of justice. Haven't you learnt anything? How can you be so blind?"

People felt pangs of guilt and were temporarily dumbfounded, but they remained angry in their hearts.

Another selected member of the audience spoke up:

"But we have no power to change things for the better!"

"Are you telling me you have no power? Do you think it goes unnoticed when you walk passed the hungry with your head held high? When you have a drink of water and see your neighbour wasting away, you rationalise your selfishness. You keep it all for yourself and assume the sufferer is unworthy of a life-saving drink."

"Wise man! Wise man! Surely human beings are composed of an intricate combination of chemicals and this chemical structure will simply alter at death and the human personality or soul will cease to exist."

"You have chosen to use intellectuality as a shield for pleading ignorance. Your lack of common sense is the consequence of deliberately washing your hands of moral responsibility in a watery solution of expertise. Tell me, why do you assume the soul does not continue beyond the death of the body simply because your text books do not choose to explore the issue? Do you only believe in what you see and feel? Just because you can't see the galaxy furthest from yours, does that mean it doesn't exist? You are playing hide and seek with your mother and you still think she can't see you because you have covered your eyes with your hands."

This was getting too much for some of the audience. They had gone to the auditorium for a quaint experience with their friends, not to be insulted. On the other hand, some members of the audience showed disapproval towards the emotional objectors, because their lack of self-control was embarrassing; so the objectors just sat down seething and muttering.

Another member of the audience asked a question:

"Wise man! Wise man! How can we know we are not simply made of chemicals that will dissolve away when we die?"

"People are not just a combination of chemicals. The human spirit is created by God inside every embryo before birth. When we interact with one another we also interact with their human soul and spirit when in their presence. It is not just the warmth of their body or the smell of their skin, but our human spirit identifying with or being repelled from their human spirit according to our personality or preferences. Such applies to our 'comfort company'. These relationships are easy. But in addition to this, we should love even our enemies, and therefore show love beyond our 'comfort company' group.

"Why do you see beauty and significance in certain people even when you have never communicated with them? Why do you feel uncomfortable in the presence of people you have never met before? Because you have a spirit and a soul, and so do they. If the spirit and soul were missing and their body was activated by a characterless and impersonal force, you would not react in the same way. A semblance of this may arise one day and you will see for yourselves.

"When you are minding your own business and suddenly look up to see someone staring right at you, is that simply a chemical reaction? Just light reflecting off someone's eyes? It is not simply their eyes engaging with you, but their soul.

"If you feel a kinship with someone, is it simply chemical processes? Look someone straight in the eyes. What do you see?

231

You see a person, a soul. You may be scared as you look because you don't know what this created being is thinking or feeling, yet you know they are a precious individual and not just a DNA sequence. You know that their thoughts and imaginings are unimaginably deep. Love is required for every soul!

"Every person is created in the womb. Not only do physical processes take place before birth, but a human spirit is also being formed, and that spirit will live in spiritual form after the body dies."

"Wise man! Wise man! What should we do?"

"The end of an era is coming. Every confusing and unexpected event points to the same thing. In the human spirit, this understanding has already been granted. We must turn around and pursue godliness."

People were afraid when the teacher told them an era was ending. What did he mean exactly?

"Wise man! Wise man! How will we know when the end has come?"

"When it is too late."

The end of the session was declared and the auditorium began to clear. Some went away feeling depressed, some determined to change their lifestyles. Others smiled and laughed about this new peculiar experience, of seeing the real wise man in the flesh, and having the experience of tension and intellectual teasers.

WATCHERS

We must be ready for the signal indicating the end of the era, whenever that may be. When the command comes in, the trumpet will sound and the removal of the chosen ones will need to be swift. They must be delivered from the coming wrath. But woe to those who are left behind on the Earth!

CHAPTER 29

The Great Removal

Two pieces of toast popped up from the silver toaster.

"Come on Trad! You'll be late for school!"

Trad ticked off another day on his chart, counting down the days until his Dad would land back safely on Earth.

"You know he won't be able to come home straight away when he lands."

"He might!" hoped Trad.

"Just don't get your hopes up, it could be months before you get to see him."

"At least he'll be safer down here."

"Don't worry, he'll get home safe and sound."

Trad went to the hall to collect his bag.

"Your bus is here!" Stel Keeper announced as she picked up their toddler Henrietta, holding her in her secure right arm, resting the child on her hip as she stood to wave him off.

'Henry' uttered a cute, "Bye".

Michael Keeper was working at the International Space Station making repairs, his family not knowing they would never again see him alive. He hardly thought of anything else besides his wife Stel, their son Trad and daughter Henry. His family were always worried about the dangers of space travel, but they trusted the engineers.

*

Arrival on Mars had been marked throughout the world as a monumental event and everyone had welled up with hope for the future of humankind. Travel by plane had become restricted to the rich and famous because of the price of fuel, but another reason was the need to facilitate and finance planetary exploration and research. The solar system had become just as unpredictable as the Earth, so astronauts were seriously at risk, but abandoning space projects would jeopardise the future of the human race which was reducing numerically at an alarming rate.

In the Mars Base, three astronauts sat round the air and moisture capsule and Jackie read out the message on the screen, 'Peculiar electrical surges are affecting satellites and communication. Assume for now you will not be able to return to Earth. President's message to follow shortly.'

"We're goners!"

"I think it's safer out here anyway."

"Yeah, well aren't you the wise one! Come on, you know they're not going to abandon their heroes! They're just covering themselves by preparing people on Earth for the worst case scenario."

"Yeah, you're right … we're goners."

"I think this news calls for a party!" said Gus standing up and wiggling his hips.

*

Those stranded on Moon Base Three had already prepared themselves for a slow, oxygen deprived death. "Seriously, we need to store as much data as possible to be retrieved later."

"Derr, you're so sensible!"

"No, just trying to keep my mind occupied. Mars has been told they are going to snuff it. The money's dried up, that's what it is! I think it's lining the pockets of the rich as usual. We are dispensable."

"Let's be fair, they are having to rebuild destroyed lives every day because of the Great Tribulation. They'll send another resource pod if they can. They're counting on us to keep the human race going in case the Earth is on its last legs."

"Good luck to 'em. Cheers, you rich killers!" said Fred pretending to raise a glass.

Down To Earth

Back on Earth, Michelle had eventually calmed down after the death of her uncle, and her little family managed to move back to Winchester, as the CEC police seemed to have forgotten about them. She began to see her uncle's death as simply another bitterly hurtful blow from life. But in spite of it all, she still felt a sense of reassurance in regard to her family as they held together and pulled through in the most terrible of circumstances. Most families didn't have a close relationship like that, so she was thankful.

Every tragedy helped her to fully appreciate how valuable and special her nuclear family was to her. Her confident character remained in spite of it all. Chris, her husband, was not always so confident, but he was a lot of fun for their little Tina. Everyone was fond of Chris and trusted him; and he was the one thing she could rely on.

That night, Michelle went to bed and slept better than she thought she would. In spite of recent events, Michelle would live for the day. After all, she had her security sleeping beside her and in the cot in the next room.

*

"Wise man! Wise man! Why is there such evil in the world?"

"Do not be anxious of tides and changes
Back and forth the swing arranges
Time in many untold ranges
Throughout history and many dangers
To these things we're never strangers
Bringing untold glory to untold ages.

"But the future is bright
As the stars at night
When all is at rest and after the fight.

"Give glory to God
His reward is in sight
Bliss and contentment, forever daylight."

*

A worldwide earthquake rumbled. People had no idea that every human being was experiencing it; this was a global event, cracking and crumbling the world. Volcanoes started to spew forth molten lava and ash billowed out of them. Forests and homes were set alight.

During this rumbling throughout the world, all sources of light went out including electrical lighting; blue skies disappeared and even the night skies became jet black. In spite of this, no stars were visible above their heads. The whole world shuddered in the cold.

*

The International Space Station was being manned by four crew. Michael Keeper and Tracey-Susan were floating around the satellite making repairs. The light had suddenly ceased to reflect from the satellite. In fact everything was black and the sun wasn't even visible.

*

The whole Earth continued to quake in the darkness. But in the falling rubble, explosions appeared, giving moments of light yet barely banishing the blackness.

*

Michael Keeper and Tracey-Susan turned round slowly from their darkened satellite. They could barely make out the Earth which had become a circular area, pin pricked with orange. A blood-red disc stood out beside it where the Moon once was.

Yet, in the distance, perhaps millions of miles away, they could see a central point of brilliant light with a shining aura. The brightness was unbelievably powerful and getting brighter. It was as though every source of light, including electrical sources on Earth, and in fact every source of light in the universe, had been sucked into that one visible sharp point of brilliance. 'This is a sign of foreboding! What's going on?' thought Michael.

The brightness was actually brighter and stronger than anyone should have been able to bear, but Michael's eyes could cope with it somehow. He floated for a while, dazed. He realised he had

238

been distracted and had forgotten about Tracey-Susan a few metres away. He spoke to her - no response! She was stunned and couldn't move. "What is this? Lord have mercy!" Michael prayed. "Could this be the end of the universe? The Second Coming? If not, it is certainly the end of me!"

*

The Mars Base collapsed into isolated molecules along with the crew and plant life inside it – all in a fraction of a second. The planet itself then exploded; pieces of the planet shot towards Earth, and debris hurtled in all directions. The fragments and debris contained secret subterranean channels and caverns never to be explored. The Asteroid Belt was also dispersed under the stress and strain of opposing forces challenging the fabric of the universe.

*

The residents of the Moon had already been crushed under a momentarily intensified gravity.

The distant point of light expanded more and more, and objects like shooting stars sprayed forth from the direction of Mars towards Michael Keeper. It looked like stars themselves were flying towards the Earth.

Michael felt even the empty space around him quaking. The satellite was a long way off now. The now glowing Earth tottered before his eyes. Unknown to him, Tracey-Susan and the satellite turned to powder.

Michael's face changed – he became radiant and drawn to the focal point of light getting ever bigger.

*

From the Earth, lights could be seen cascading towards them. Meteors hit various parts of the Earth increasing the explosions and fires already bursting forth due to the Earth's quaking. A glow began to spread across the whole sky.

*

From his position, Michael saw a halo of light surrounding the Earth, but the Moon remained a foreboding blood-red colour.

*

The screams of those on Earth echoed throughout the globe. Some cried out to God, others simply cried out, as the worldwide glow intensified, surrounding the entire globe like a giant spotlight analysing every crack, crinkle and wrinkle, exposing everything before a heavenly audience. All flesh quaked, human and animal. Some people knelt down, others curled into a ball, others stood tall, some raised their hands and lifted their heads expecting redemption. Wherever they stood, crawled or walked, there was no escape from the One who could see into every heart.

The electric lights came back on, and for those where the earthquake was least powerful, it was business as usual, some working indoors, some outdoors, but the internet and other forms of communication were down.

*

After some hours, angelic beings began to visibly fly around in the sky. Some darted to and fro, and the human race watched with terrified faces. Even in the streets, people began to notice human-like beings walking around, some appearing with awesome faces, glowing and dressed in white. Some of these beings were even seen in people's houses.

Suddenly, countless angels saturated planet Earth. To add to the foreboding, the huge blood-red Moon above stood out even more against the white backdrop, but the Sun was still not visible.

Then, angels' voices rang out, summoning the heavenly beings for action. A continuous loud trumpet blast was heard by all.

*

In space, Michael was floating towards the light. It began to look like an immense glowing cloud from which he could hear a deafening sound. As he floated towards the cloud, he saw something like a person in the middle, how big he did not know.

240

He felt himself smiling, his fear dissipating as his emotions became heavenly, perfect, with inexpressible joy, a peace and assurance, a pure sense of home. His body started to shine like the glow from the brilliance of the light. He was being taken, but he did not mind – it just felt right! His body changed; it became imperishable, incorruptible.

The chosen ones all over the world began to be taken up by angels to be delivered from a crumbling world to remain with their Creator in safety and bliss.

*

Michelle's dreams became more agitated. A powerful light shone before her as she slept, and in the centre was what seemed to be a human-like being. Burning lights flew at her while glowing lights were also drawn towards the figure in the middle. A piercing noise reached her ears from the light, growing in intensity, like a deafening signal. Everything around her quaked. She sat up in bed and exited her dream. However, everything around her continued to shake! She got out of bed and ran to the window only to see something she could not believe – people strewn across the street, buildings wrecked, dust everywhere.

"Chris! Chris! What's going on? I'm having a horrible dream!" A sound assaulted her ears, the sound of people all over the world moaning, groaning and wailing like a chorus from Hell. "Chris! Chris! It's awful!" She looked back towards the bed. Her husband was gone!

Narrator

The end of an era has come; the world was warned time and time again. In spite of this, many were not prepared. Only the chosen ones will be saved. Who will the Creator leave behind? What will become of them?

Meanwhile, the Beast and the Dragon are spectating, awaiting and mulling over the events surely to come. They have an awareness of future events and have plans that they are ready to put into action for the world's remaining inhabitants.

<u>Acknowledgments</u>

<u>*Cover Design*</u>

Andrew Harrison   *Copyright 2018*

Printed in Great Britain
by Amazon

86747091R00139